Max walked i[n]

Abbey shook her [...] don't report to Ja[ne ...] here and we'll be c[...]

'And that might cause a scandal?' he asked provocatively.

Aware that her cheeks were flaming, Abbey snapped, 'Don't be so silly—'

'If it makes you feel better,' he interrupted quietly, 'I did report to Jane.'

'So why didn't she ring through to announce you?'

'I told her not to. Old friends like us don't need such formality. Don't you agree?'

Born in the industrial north, **Sheila Danton** trained as a registered general nurse in London before joining the Air Force nursing service. Her career was interrupted by marriage, three children, and a move to the West Country, where she now lives. She soon returned to her chosen career, training and specialising in occupational health, with an interest in preventive medicine. Sheila has now taken early retirement, and is thrilled to be able to write full time.

Recent titles by the same author:

PRESCRIPTION FOR CHANGE
MONSOONS APART
BASE PRINCIPLES
DANGEROUS PRACTICE
SHARED RESPONSIBILITY

A PRIVATE AFFAIR

BY
SHEILA DANTON

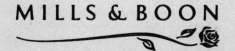

MILLS & BOON

MILLS & BOON, the Rose Device and
LOVE ON CALL are trademarks of the publisher.
Harlequin Mills & Boon Limited,
Eton House, 18-24 Paradise Road, Richmond, Surrey TW9 1SR

© Sheila Danton 1996

ISBN 0 263 79602 7

Set in Times 10 on 11 pt. by
Rowland Phototypesetting Limited
Bury St Edmunds, Suffolk

03-9606-49755

Made and printed in Great Britain
Cover illustration by Brian Denington

CHAPTER ONE

THROUGH her slightly open door, Abbey Westray could hear the deep, insistent voice demanding to see her immediately.

'I'm sorry.' Jane, her secretary, was trying unsuccessfully to persuade the speaker it wasn't possible. 'This is the manager's first morning and she can't be disturbed at the moment.'

'When she hears what I have to say, she *will* be,' the gruff voice retorted.

'I could make an appointment for you later this afternoon,' Jane replied soothingly. 'How about—?'

'Far too late,' the invisible voice interrupted. 'This is an emergency.'

Irritated, Abbey snatched open her door, then took a hasty step back from the familiar figure filling the narrow corridor.

She should have recognised the voice, but it must have been getting on for ten years since this man's rugged features had first made such an impression on her.

A nurse by training, she was well aware that it wasn't going to be easy to establish her authority as manager of a private hospital, but the sight of Max Darby's impressive physique, revealed only too clearly by the closely fitting theatre greens he wore, made Abbey fear that inexperience was going to be the least of her problems.

He strode confidently towards her, his arms outstretched. 'How good to see you again, Abbey.'

He swung her petite frame off the ground and held her at arm's length so that he could inspect her features

5

from every angle, finally allowing his dark eyes to meet the challenge of her gaze. 'You haven't changed one little bit.'

Conscious of Jane's amused glance, she freed herself from the grasp of his enormous hands and said curtly, 'I've changed more than you think, Mr Darby. I'm no longer the nurse you remember. I'm the new manager of St Luke's. I gather from all the commotion that you want to see me about something important.' Reluctantly tearing her gaze away, she led the way into her room, closing the door behind him.

An engaging grin crinkled his dark eyes as she smoothed the skirt of her neat navy suit and seated herself behind the desk.

'Does that mean I have to call you Abigail these days, or Miss Westray even?' He sat down on the chair opposite so that she couldn't avoid meeting his eyes again.

Sure that he had deliberately emphasised the 'Miss', Abbey said firmly, 'I have a lot of work to get through today, so if you could just tell me about your emergency as quickly as possible—'

He didn't let her finish. 'All in good time. I need first to discover how much you know about running an acute hospital of this size.'

'That information was offered at my interview and obviously met with approval or I wouldn't be here. I don't think we need to go into it again today. I'd appreciate it if you'd tell me about your problem as quickly as possible.'

Abbey knew that she must sound prissy but seeing him so unexpectedly had thrown her, especially when she hadn't had a chance to find her way around the paperwork waiting on her desk.

She half expected him to retaliate in a similar fashion, but he didn't speak immediately. Rather, he

examined her from between narrowed lids as she
waited, pen and paper at the ready.

'I'm not sure I like your hair short. I prefer those
luxuriant tresses I used to run my fingers through.'

She'd been warned at the interview that she would
have to be firm with the medical staff as they thought
the hospital was run for their benefit. But, before she
could do that, she needed to earn their respect, and
preventing Max from taking liberties would be a
good start.

Unconsciously smoothing her short blonde curls, she
said, 'Just tell me what you came to say. I've a
lot to do.'

He met the steely gaze of her blue eyes with equa-
nimity. 'This hospital is regularly losing business due
to the non-co-operation of the theatre department.'

Abbey's eyes widened suspiciously. 'In what way?'

'We are restricted as to when we can operate. There
are insufficient theatre staff for them to be flexible
over the scheduling. Business people pay for their
operations to be done at a time convenient to them.
If it can't be arranged here they'll go elsewhere and
the surgeons will follow.'

'The medics committee is the place to discuss this
and any similar problems. It is certainly not a priority
on my first day in this post.'

Max raised a doubting eyebrow. 'It is when Mr
Renny is down there at the moment wanting to do
a simple hernia repair and he's been told there are
insufficient nurses available!'

'Is it an emergency?' Abbey asked brusquely.

'Well, not exactly,' he admitted. 'But the time is
convenient both to the patient and Mr Renny. And
the patient is already admitted here. It won't look too
good to throw him out unrepaired!'

To give herself time to work out an answer, Abbey
made a note of his complaints on her pad.

Determined not to allow her the chance to argue, he continued, 'If you can't find a way to do this for the surgeon he'll soon be on his way down the road, and, I can tell you, he'll be received with open arms at the Cotswold. You have a lot of competition in Bleasdon, you know.'

'I'm well aware of that,' Abbey told him shortly. 'But what has all this to do with you?'

'You mean you don't know?' He quirked an amused eyebrow. 'I'm the new chairperson of the medics committee.'

'You mean—' Abbey's heart plummeted as she grasped the implications of his statement '—you mean you've replaced Gordon Glennie?'

Aware of the need to work closely with the chairman of the MedCom, Abbey had been pleased to discover at her interview that she and Gordon appeared to be on the same wavelength.

'That's about it. Now, what are you going to do about Mr Renny's patient?'

'Nothing until I find out what's happening from the theatre sister and can assess the overall situation. I'll get back to you and Mr Renny as soon as I can. In the meantime, perhaps you'd explain to him that this is my first day.' She rose from her seat and moved towards the door, indicating that their discussion was over.

Instead of taking the hint and leaving, he looked her up and down before saying, 'I remember you were a damn fine theatre nurse. You could assist me with an arthroscopy, freeing the other nurse to scrub for the hernia.'

Trying to ignore the pleasure that spread through her at his compliment, Abbey shook her head. 'How do you think it'll look if the new hospital manager scrubs up on her first day?'

'It'll look as if you've got the business *and* the

patients' interests at heart. And that you are willing to get your hands dirty.'

While conceding that it might possibly help towards her acceptance as hospital manager, Abbey was also aware that it might do just the opposite. And the last thing she wanted to do was to upset the theatre staff, who were crucial to the organisation.

'If it can be done at the Cotswold I think that'd be the best way, until I can sort out the staffing situation.'

Max glared at her, his dark eyes wide with antagonism.

'That's the way to lose business. Once Tom Renny's inveigled in there, we might not see him again. They're as desperate to attract paying business as we are.'

When she didn't answer, he continued, 'I thought you were engaged to change the fortunes of this place. Please yourself, but under the circumstances I know what I'd do.'

To prevent herself being steamrollered against her will, she retorted, 'Apart from anything else, I'm out of practice clinically.' He didn't need to know about the hard work she'd put in to keep her nursing registration up to date whilst studying for her management qualification.

'You can work with me—there'll be no problem. Let Helen assist Tom.'

'Helen?' Abbey queried, 'I don't think I've met—'

'Helen Baker. In charge of Theatres. Surely you at least know all the departmental managers?'

Abbey nodded. 'All but Miss Baker. She was on leave when I did my orientation tour.'

'You'd better come down now and I'll introduce you.'

Determined to make a stand, Abbey resisted firmly. 'I'm afraid I have more important things to attend to today.'

Max raised a sceptical eyebrow. 'More important than saving this business from going down the pan? I doubt it.'

Abbey would have sent him packing then and there if they hadn't been interrupted by a red-haired girl opening the door cautiously, 'Sorry to interrupt, but—'

'Helen.' Max drew her forward. 'Come and meet the new manager. She's theatre-trained and willing to help us out of this spot.'

Abbey opened her mouth to protest but apparently oblivious, Max continued, 'She can assist me, Helen, leaving you free to cope with Tom Renny's herniorrhaphy.'

'Er. . .I'm not sure if. . .' Helen's voiced tailed off mid-sentence as Max threw her a warning glance.

'I can't see any problem. It's no different from employing an agency nurse who doesn't know our set-up.'

'I suppose not,' Helen said doubtfully.

'Right. That's settled. I'll go and tell Tom.'

Recognising that his solution hadn't made the theatre sister any happier than she herself was, Abbey was furious that Max had prevented her from saying so. Well aware from her own experience that each scrub nurse had her own preferences amongst the surgeons, Abbey guessed that Mr Renny was not one of Helen's favourites.

'You're going far too fast, Max,' she snapped. 'I need to explore all the options with *my* staff before I allow myself to be railroaded into something I might regret. Perhaps you'd leave us to sort this out.'

He shrugged. 'OK. But I can tell you. There's no other option. Right, Sister?'

Helen didn't speak until the door had closed behind him. 'I'm afraid he's right. We haven't the nurses available to call in, and those we do have can't work miracles.'

'Why are you so short-staffed?'

'Your predecessor wouldn't allow any recruitment.' She hesitated, obviously nervous. 'It would certainly help us out of a spot if you could do as Mr Darby suggested, but—that is, do you have current registration?'

Abbey nodded. 'I've kept my hand in with agency work, just in case I want to return to the practical side.' She sighed. 'I can see it might help you this time. But what about tomorrow? And the next day? If it *was* a one-off emergency, I'd be only too happy to step in. But it doesn't sound to me as if there's any chance of the situation improving in the short term.'

Helen shrugged. 'One of our best scrub nurses returns from annual leave tomorrow, which will ease things for the time being. Until someone goes off sick. Which is more than likely with the overtime they're having to put in.'

Abbey remained silent as she turned the problem over in her mind. Eventually deciding that the last thing she wanted was to be seen as being negative, she uttered on a sigh of resignation, 'OK. If it'll help, I'll do it this once.'

'Did Mr Darby tell you that it's his brother-in-law waiting for the hernia repair?'

Abbey raised her eyes to the heaven. 'I should have guessed there was more to it than concern for the business.' She should have known by now that Max Darby only ever had his own interests at heart. 'What's his brother-in-law's name?' she asked, wondering if they'd met during her brief relationship with Max all those years ago.

'Peter Barnes. He's a financial adviser and has sorted out pension problems for quite a few of the staff.'

Although sure she didn't know him, Abbey grinned. 'It gets worse! If the whole hospital is rooting for him, we'd better not waste another moment.'

As she and Helen made their way down to the theatre changing rooms, Abbey said, 'I'll look into the staffing levels as soon as I can but I've a pile of paper-work to get through before I can assess the situation overall.'

Helen nodded. 'I'm not expecting permanent staff. I'd just like to recruit a few more for our nurse bank so that when problems arise we have more chance of finding someone not already booked to work elsewhere.'

Sensing that Helen might be a useful ally in the future, Abbey suggested, 'Come and discuss this with me tomorrow afternoon. Hopefully I'll be coming up from under the deluge of paperwork by that time.'

When Abbey emerged from the changing room in theatre greens, the satisfied smile that flitted across Max's features almost made her change her mind. But not quite. He might have got his own way this time but he needn't expect it on a regular basis!

Over the years their careers has taken divergent paths, and he'd probably never given her a second thought. But at least he'd recognised her, so perhaps, for old times' sake, he would try and prevent his col-leagues from making things too difficult as she adapted to her new role.

However, for the moment she must forget her worries about management and concentrate on the job in hand.

As she checked the trolley Helen had already pre-pared for the arthroscopy the familiar aura of the operating theatre closed round her, boosting her confidence.

Relieved to discover that the instruments laid out were similar to those she was used to, her blue eyes roved around the most modern theatre she'd ever worked in. Above her mask, her eyes widened at the amount of equipment she'd never seen before—most of it, no doubt, there to make life easier for the staff.

'Who's anaesthetising?' she asked.

'John Browning.'

She didn't know him so she popped her head round the anaesthetic-room door to introduce herself. 'I'd hoped to meet the patient while he was still conscious but I see I'm too late.'

John Browning nodded as he completed injecting an intravenous anaesthetic.

While Abbey watched, John and his assistant quickly inserted a tube to maintain the patient's airway throughout the operation.

Leaving them to their duties, she returned to the theatre. 'What's the patient's name?' she asked Max as she joined him at the washbasins. 'He doesn't look very old.'

'Denny Dale. He's a keen local footballer with knee problems. I think the joint's probably had such ill treatment that there are loose bodies around. I'm hoping to get away with tidying up the cartilage and removing any bits and pieces.'

By the time they were gowned and gloved and ready to start, the anaesthetised patient had been wheeled in on his bed. He was then transferred to the table with a device that latched onto the canvas poles, enabling the patient to be moved with little strain on the staff.

Abbey raised her eyebrows at Max. 'That must reduce the number of theatre nurses with bad backs.'

Above his mask, she saw his eyes lighten with a grin. 'And surgeons!'

As she handed him the sterile drapes she murmured, 'The new lifting regulations have certainly made a difference to hospital staff.'

He nodded and, having prepared the site, silently held his hand out for a scalpel. Abbey was amused that, despite the passage of years, he expected her to know exactly what he wanted without asking.

The incision having been made, she anticipated his every need until he told her, 'I'm ready for the arthroscope now.'

As Abbey handed him the fibre-optic tube that would allow him to have a good look inside the joint their eyes met, and the look in his sent a shock wave scudding along her veins that told her only too clearly that her feelings for him hadn't diminished with the years.

'As I expected, debris to be cleared,' Max murmured. 'Forceps.'

His concentration on what he was doing was total, and Abbey felt a painful twist of her heart as she watched his skilful hands. The operation was soon over and, as he asked for the suture he required, she was conscious of his eyes watching her with a definite query in them.

Snipping the sutures neatly, she was secretly delighted by the way she and Max could still work together as a team. As they stripped off their gloves and gowns he nodded appreciatively. 'You've certainly not lost any of your expertise. Let's hope your management skills are as sharp, though why you want to shuffle paper when you could be doing this I can't imagine.'

'You wouldn't understand. Every day you see patients getting better as a result of your treatment. As a theatre nurse I felt I was achieving nothing.'

'That's rubbish. Every successful operation can only take place with a good scrub nurse to help.'

'Maybe, but I rarely heard what happened to the patients once they left the theatre. So I had to be satisfied with the knowledge that I'd done my job well enough for the consultant not to throw any instruments back at me!'

'As if we would.' Well aware that he'd done it himself in the past when things weren't going right, Max gave her a sheepish grin. 'However, I would have thought even that was more worthwhile than what you're doing now.'

'Well, I don't.' Resentful of his criticism, she handed the patient over to the recovery suite staff and headed for the changing room.

'I do hope the operation on your brother-in-law is going as smoothly, Max,' she called over her shoulder, giving him no chance to reply as the door closed behind her. She slipped out of the theatre greens with a smile on her face. One up to her. He'd thought that she didn't know the identity of the patient he'd made the fuss over.

After glancing at her appearance in the mirror she made her way back to her office.

Jane was still working at her word processor. 'Mr Darby's not an easy man to deal with, is he?' She giggled. 'I thought for a moment that he was going to pick me up from behind the desk and use me as a battering ram to get to you.'

Abbey shook her head ruefully. 'He always has been determined to get his own way, and his size usually prevents anyone arguing with him.' She laughed. 'But you needn't worry; I don't believe he's ever assaulted anyone other than verbally.'

Jane shook her head. 'All the same, it's a pity you didn't start when Gordon Glennie was still chairman of the committee. You could reason with him.'

Abbey nodded, 'I couldn't agree more.'

'You did notice tonight's meeting of the MedCom entered in your diary, didn't you?' Jane asked, flicking through some files.

'Don't worry, I'll be there.' Abbey went back into her own room and shut the door, firmly this time. After helping herself to a cup of coffee from the filter machine on her desk, she sighed deeply and lifted the pile of papers left by her predecessor.

As she read she discovered that the hospital's
finances appeared to be in a more parlous state than
she'd been led to believe at the interview. It was only
too clear why the previous manager had reduced the
staffing levels. No one could afford to spend out money
on salaries when the work wasn't coming in.

By five o'clock her head was befuddled by figures
and she longed for a quiet evening at home. However,
she still had to meet Max Darby and his committee of
consultants. They would no doubt expect her to come
up with possible solutions to the hospital's problems
even though she had only started work that day.

She waited for Jane to lock up and they walked
down to the committee room together.

A few minutes later, when the committee members
were seated and all was quiet, Max said, 'I called this
meeting so that we could all meet—er—Ms Westray.'

'I prefer "Miss",' she corrected him.

'So that we could meet *Miss* Westray,' he stressed.
'As you know, I didn't have the pleasure of being at
her interview, so, on behalf of us all, I'd like to offer
her a warm welcome to St Luke's.'

Abbey thanked him and added, 'I look forward to
us all working together for the good of the hospital.'

His dark eyes glittered. 'So do I. So do I.' He turned
to the remaining members of the committee. 'Perhaps
you'd each like to introduce yourself and your special-
ity. We'll start with you, Tom.'

'Tom Renny, general surgeon.'

'Jeff Turnbull, Plastics.'

As each consultant followed suit, Abbey listened
carefully, taking a special note of those that the group
chairman had warned her could be troublemakers.

When they'd finished, Max enquired, 'Shall we go
on to discuss last month's figures?'

Knowing the hospital had made a loss for the past

three months, Abbey guessed that this was where she would need to make her first stand. 'I gather the number of operations regularly falls at this time of year.'

Max's sceptically raised eyebrow spoke volumes. 'I have to admit that Christmas and the New Year is always a quiet period in private practice, but this year has been particularly bad at St Luke's and we're looking to you to find ways of reversing the trend.'

Abbey sucked in a lungful of air before declaring, 'As far as I can see there are probably several reasons for this. But until I've had time to go through the figures more thoroughly I'm not prepared to speculate on how to improve things. However—' she smiled as she looked round the assembled doctors '—I promise I'll get back to your chairman before the end of the week with some answers.'

'We quite understand, Miss Westray, and look forward to hearing from you.' Abbey remembered from the old days the enigmatic smile that was hovering round Max's lips as he spoke and, deciding that he was merely humouring her, waited for his next onslaught.

However, the refreshments arrived from the hospital kitchen at that moment and, pleasantly surprised by the spread provided, she watched Max rise from his seat to join the other consultants.

There was still not an inch of spare flesh on his muscular frame and breathlessly aware of his attraction for her, Abbey dragged her attention back to what the consultant on her left was saying.

'The facilities here are second to none,' he told her ingratiatingly, 'so it ought not to be difficult to attract more business.'

Ignoring what she decided was an attempt to belittle her position, Abbey smiled sweetly as she told him, 'I'm glad you approve of what we have to offer. I look forward to your continued co-operation.'

Over coffee, Abbey circulated, taking careful note of the many minor grievances voiced by some of the consultants. Max ignored her completely, and though she knew she ought to be grateful it piqued her that he was openly showering his attentions on the only female doctor in the room, Ellie Wycliffe, the hospital's resident medical officer.

Eventually the room emptied, until only her secretary and a member of the catering staff remained.

Abbey smiled at the young lad, whose eyes were almost hidden beneath his chef's hat. 'Thank you. The food was obviously appreciated.' She gestured towards the array of empty plates.

Jane grinned. 'I sometimes think these consultants never get a meal at home. They eat anything and everything.' She collected together her papers. 'If you don't need me, Miss Westray, I'll get back and type up these minutes.'

'Fine. I'll come with you. And please don't feel you have to call me Miss Westray. I'm Abbey to my friends.'

As they walked along the corridor Jane frowned. 'You said in there that you wanted to be known as Miss Westray.'

Abbey laughed. 'I needed to exert my authority over the consultants before they all tried to take advantage of a manager whom some of them remember as a nurse. I think it worked, as well. The one I feared most, Mr Darby, was definitely thrown off his stride.'

They were still laughing as they reached their respective offices at the top of the building. 'You won't stay too late, will you, Jane? It's already after eight.'

'I just want to get the gist of the minutes down before I forget. It won't take long.'

'Right. I'm off home now. You'll lock up when you leave, won't you?'

Heavy footsteps sounded on the stairs. Not expecting

anyone to visit the offices at that time of night, they both watched curiously. When Max rounded the corner, Jane hurried into her own office and closed the door.

'Can you spare a moment, Abbey?'

She opened her office door and ushered him inside, but left the door open.

'You didn't really enjoy it down there, did you? You're a bloody good nurse. What on earth set you on this career path? It's not for you.'

Abbey was indignant. 'You don't know anything about me these days, Max. I told you, I'm not the same person.'

'What changed you, then? Was it that guy you shacked up with the moment I turned my back?'

Unable to believe what she was hearing, Abbey protested, 'How dare you suggest. . .?'

She paused, searching for the right words to explain, but he didn't give her a chance to find them. 'Oh, I dare. I thought we were old friends, but you tried to make a fool of me back there. Miss Abigail Westray indeed!'

'Surely you can understand I needed to establish my authority? This job isn't going to be easy.'

He shook his head disbelievingly. 'You *have* changed. Where's the fun-loving girl I remember? Hidden behind that hard exterior? Or extinguished by ambition?' His eyes glittered angrily. 'Well, I agree with you that the job won't be easy, because there are changes needed here—vast changes—and, now I'm chairman, I'm going to see that they happen, even if I have to fight you every inch of the way.'

Abbey guessed that she must have looked as washed out as she felt at that moment, for he suddenly barked out, 'Have you eaten today?'

She nodded. 'At the meeting—'

'You mean those titbits are all you've had? You

can't work these kind of hours on an empty stomach. You'd better join me for a meal.'

She glared at him. 'I can't do that, I'm afraid. I'm eating with the guy I "shacked up with", as you so delicately put it.'

'And he still hasn't given you a wedding ring?' he queried scathingly, before turning abruptly on his heels and striding off at speed.

A slow smile spread across her face as she packed away her files. He didn't need to know that Ben and his wife had asked her to dinner as a thank-you for Abbey's repeated help when relapses made the symptoms of Ben's multiple sclerosis unmanageable. Let Max think what he wanted. It made no difference now.

He hadn't cared enough to keep in touch when his house job had finished all those years ago. She'd been young and gullible and had made a complete fool of herself over him. But it hadn't been totally unproductive. It was partly his behaviour that had decided her to aim for a position in her career that was not subservient to the medical staff.

And now that she'd arrived she didn't intend to throw all her hard work away, however unchanged her feelings were for him. If she wasn't to make a fool of herself all over again, she would perhaps find it easier if he believed that she already had a partner.

On a sudden impulse Abbey made her way to the day-case ward and, having introduced herself, enquired of the nurse in charge of the shift whether Mr Renny's hernia had gone home as yet.

'Any minute now. His wife's just packing his things up, ready for Mr Darby to collect them.'

'Which room?'

'Thirty-two.'

'And Denny Dale? How's he?'

The nurse laughed. 'Far too active and after every nurse that comes within his reach.'

'When he sees me he'll change his tune.' Abbey grinned. 'Which room is he in?'

'The end. Number one.'

'Thanks.' Abbey made her way down the corridor to Room 32. 'Hello, Mr Barnes. I'm the manager here and just wanted to check that you're feeling well enough to leave.'

A fresh-faced girl turned and grinned at her. 'You just started today?' At Abbey's nod, the girl rushed on, 'Max told us how grateful we should be to you. Apparently the op couldn't have been done if you hadn't rolled up your sleeves to help. We're very grateful.'

'No problem. I actually enjoyed it. I hope everything continues to go well with Mr Barnes.'

'I'm sure it will.' It was the patient who answered this time. 'I must say, the treatment here has been first-class. I'm very grateful to you and to all your staff. They've been marvellous.'

'I'm pleased to hear it.' She shook hands with them both. 'All the best and don't try and do too much too soon.' She closed the door behind her and, not wanting to meet up with Max again, nodded her thanks to the senior nurse and made her way to Denny's room.

As she entered he was reaching across to catch the arm of a young nurse who was leaving his bedside.

'Hello, Denny.'

He was leaning too far out of bed and, at the sound of an unexpected voice, nearly fell the whole way. Abbey caught him and, with the nurse, helped him back into an upright position. He looked up with a cheeky grin. 'Who're you?'

'The hospital manager. Come on, now, let's get you comfortable.'

'You! But you're a manager.'

She laughed. 'So I am, but I did assist Mr Darby with your operation.'

He stared at her with open-mouthed disbelief. 'You didn't.'

She laughed. 'I'm a theatre-trained nurse as well.'

He joined in the laughter then. 'That's all right, then.'

'Now lie still and leave my nurses alone or you'll do that knee some mischief.'

'OK, ma'am,' he told her seriously, and, trying not to laugh, Abbey left him in the nurse's care, wondering what he would get up to when he was discharged the next day.

Wearily she made her way up the stairs before locking her office and heading for the relative peacefulness of her friends' home.

'How's it gone?' Ben's wife greeted her.

'Not the way I expected. But OK.' She sniffed appreciatively. 'What a delicious smell, Cheryl.'

'It's only a lamb stew. Come on and tell us all about your day.'

'Only?' Abbey was strangely reluctant to talk about meeting up with Max again. 'This is a real treat on my first day.'

'I can see that until we've fed you you're not going to talk about anything but food.'

'Don't blame her.' Despite his illness making speech difficult for him, Ben was determined not to be left out of their conversation.

Abbey thoroughly enjoyed her meal, and was relieved to get away without having had to go into too many details of what had felt like the longest day she'd ever worked.

Despite sleeping heavily that night she was in the office early, hoping for the uninterrupted morning she'd been denied the previous day.

She was deeply immersed in her paperwork when Jane came in with the morning's mail. Abbey dealt with the most urgent and put the rest aside to attend to when she had a spare moment. If she ever found one! The way things were going she doubted it, especially when there was a loud knock on her door the moment her secretary left.

Not exactly pleased, Abbey looked up as, without waiting for an invitation, the theatre manager burst in.

'Good morning,' Abbey greeted her frostily. 'I thought our appointment was for this afternoon. I—'

Unhappily, Helen interrupted, 'I'm afraid what I have to say can't wait. If we go on at this rate we'll be doing no operations at all.'

CHAPTER TWO

ABBEY'S eyes remained cold as she said, 'You'd better sit down, Helen. But make it brief.'

'You've got to authorise immediate recruitment. We need more staff, and urgently. I'm being pressurised to book in more cases than I can cope with. The plastic surgeons say they're losing out to the gynae men, who always protest their ops are urgent.'

Abbey regarded her levelly for a few moments, then said, 'I thought you said your best scrub nurse was back from leave today.'

'She is, but two others have reported sick. We can't go on like this.'

'Until I've had a chance to go through the business plan, I'm not authorising anything.'

Unable to meet Abbey's eyes for long, Helen turned her head to the window. 'It's your fault,' she muttered petulantly. 'What you did yesterday has made the situation worse.'

Abbey couldn't believe her ears. 'In what way?'

Heedless of the manager's icy tone, Helen rushed on, 'Having heard what happened, the consultants are making impossible demands. They can't see now why we can't be more flexible for everyone.'

Abbey sighed: this was what she had feared and had hoped Helen would be able to handle. 'I'll speak to them. When's the best time to arrange a meeting?'

Helen laughed nervously. 'It's an impossibility to get them all together. During the day they're scattered around too many different hospitals. But don't worry, I'll send the worst complainers to your door.' She turned and hurried from the room, obviously relieved, and Abbey had the sudden feeling that she was being manipulated.

Jane popped her head round the door. 'Er—Mr Darby is demanding an audience. As soon as possible. What time shall I tell him?'

'Surprise, surprise. I guessed Helen's visit wasn't her own idea.' Exasperated, Abbey banged down the file she was holding. 'This is ridiculous, Jane. Until I can get to grips with all this, I can't make any decisions. Tell him I can't see anybody for the rest of the day.'

Jane raised an eyebrow. 'I'll try, but he's determined.'

'No doubt, but so am I.'

The secretary grinned. 'The last manager had similar trouble. Helen and Mr Darby are thick as thieves. She's probably sent him up here to put pressure on you.'

'Hmm, maybe, but I can't help wondering if *he* sent *her*. I wonder if I'm missing something?'

'In what way?'

'Is it possible that their relationship is more than a working one?'

Jane shrugged noncommittally. 'They're both free agents.'

In a bid to hide her surprise that Max had not been snapped up long ago, Abbey smiled. 'That's something to be thankful for at least.' She was only too aware that in a small organisation like St Luke's extramarital relationships among the staff had the potential to create havoc.

'I suppose I'd better see him. But tell him—impress on him—that I can only spare five minutes at most.'

Two seconds later Max strode into the room without knocking and handed her the largest bouquet she had ever seen.

As the colour flooded into her cheeks, she read

the card. 'Thank you for everything. Pete and Melissa Barnes.'

Relieved that she'd caught sight of the card before she made a fool of herself, Abbey was about to enquire after the patient when Max took her breath away by throwing the draft of an advertisement for theatre staff on her desk. 'Helen needs these staff now. Recruitment takes time. For goodness' sake, get the ad out immediately.'

Determined not to give in to their combined pressure as she had the day before, Abbey pushed the rough draft carelessly to one side and said, 'Mr Darby—'

'What do you mean, "Mr Darby"?' he interrupted. 'What's wrong with Max?'

Abbey folded her arms determinedly across her chest. 'Mr Darby, the operating theatre is not the only department in this hospital. Until I'm left in peace to discover the overall picture, I'm changing nothing.'

'I told you yesterday—you won't have a business then.'

Abbey retorted, 'You know as well as I do that a couple more days won't make that much difference. Just give me a chance.'

He pulled up a chair and, seating himself, leaned towards her. 'Abbey, you're being unreasonable. Come on. Surely you can see how much more could be done if only you'd agree. Do it for old times' sake,' he coaxed. 'One little ad isn't going to make that much difference to the budget, surely?'

'If I give in, that's the start of a slippery slope. If I allow more theatre staff and more operations are done, we could have problems with insufficient ward staff. You consultants will be the first to complain if the patients are not looked after to your satisfaction once they arrive back on the ward. Now, leave me in peace to find out the true picture for myself, please.'

Max rose from his chair and shook his head in

apparent disgust. 'Wasting your life on a man who lacks commitment must be enough to harden the softest heart.'

He strode out and slammed the door, leaving Abbey to grin wryly to herself. If only he knew. It was *his* lack of commitment all those years ago that had done the damage. He was the one person she *would* have abandoned her career plans for. Instead, his behaviour had fuelled them.

Much to her relief, she was left alone for the remainder of the day, and by seven she had a much clearer grasp of what was happening and was even beginning to see what she might be able to do to improve the situation.

Pleased with her day's work, she stowed the papers away in her filing cabinet and, after locking her door, made her way down to the front entrance.

As she reached the bottom of the stairs, she saw Max and Helen leaving the building, laughing and joking.

So Jane was right. As she watched them leave the car park together in his dark blue BMW, Abbey smiled to herself. Now she knew for sure, it would be much easier to handle the situation.

Or so she thought, until the tiniest shaft of jealousy pierced her heart. Annoyed because she was determined not to allow her emotions to rule her head as she had all those years ago, Abbey returned to her flat in a restless mood and immersed herself in housework to try and rid herself of the feeling.

The next day she made a determined effort to find time to go round and chat with each of the in-patients and see how they felt about their treatment at the hospital. She was pleased with what she heard until she encountered one of Max's patients.

'I'm going on fine now, but I had to have the hip replacement done when the hospital could fit me in rather than when I wanted it. Later rather than sooner, if you see what I mean.'

Frowning, Abbey explained, 'I'm sorry to hear that, Mr Murray. We do have a large number of surgeons working here, so obviously the theatre is not always available when requested. However, we do our best to fit in with everyone's wishes. I'm sorry that we didn't succeed in your case.'

The patient grinned. 'Actually, it was more of a problem for Mr Darby than for me.'

'When did you actually have the new hip?'

'Last Friday.'

'So you're getting around now?'

'Too true. And without pain. I can still hardly believe it.'

Abbey smiled. 'Hip replacement is about the only operation where most patients say they have less pain immediately after the op than before. It's like a little miracle.'

'I couldn't agree more. I haven't moved so freely for years.'

Having reassured herself that he was happy with his care since the operation, she made her way thought-fully to the ward office.

Penny, the ward sister, wasn't at all surprised to hear what Mr Murray had had to say. 'It's a common complaint from many of Mr Darby's patients. I think he puts them up to it.'

Abbey shrugged. 'It wouldn't surprise me. Did Mr Murray have to wait long, do you know?'

Penny laughed. 'From the time he saw Mr Darby in Outpatients? A week at the most, I should think. As you know, we haven't been that busy.'

Pushing the complaint to the back of her mind, Abbey concentrated on ascertaining the number of extra ward staff that Penny thought would be necessary if the theatres increased their throughput.

'It depends what kind of case they do. If they're day cases we should manage, but if they're going to need longer nursing it could be a problem.'

'So if I advertise for staff for the theatre bank, will you need some as well?'

Penny shook her head. 'We have plenty to call on at the moment. We've built up a large bank and we use them reasonably regularly, which means we don't need as many contract staff.'

Abbey nodded, pleased to learn that at least someone was satisfied. She returned to her office and asked Helen to come and see her. 'I've had a chat with Penny and have decided I'm not going to agree to any permanent recruitment for the time being. However, I see no harm in advertising to increase the number of uncontracted theatre staff for you to call on when necessary.'

'That's something. It'll be great to have a few more on the bank. Theatre nurses are in demand everywhere so at the moment I usually find that those already on the bank have been booked elsewhere.'

Abbey wondered why Helen thought that the newly recruited theatre nurses would be any more available than those she was already in contact with, but she didn't voice her doubts. If appointing non-contract staff took the pressure off the situation for the time being, she'd be more than grateful.

So she said, 'Perhaps you'd like to draft an ad and leave it with Jane.'

Helen's cheeks coloured prettily. 'Didn't Mr Darby leave one with you yesterday?'

Abbey riffled through her papers as if she hadn't given it another thought. 'I believe he did. You've seen it, then?'

Helen nodded. 'I told him I thought it sounded fine. If there's nothing else I'd better get back to the department.' She scurried from the office with evident relief.

Abbey shook her head as she watched Helen leave. Although she now knew for certain that they'd colluded over the advertisement the day before, she was sure that she had resolved that problem for the time being.

So she was totally unprepared for Max storming in to see her later that afternoon.

'Helen tells me she's only allowed to recruit bank staff.'

'That's right,' Abbey informed him coldly, wondering if every time she gave a little he would be pushing for more, 'but I don't see what it has to do with you.'

'It's not good enough.'

'I have already explained my reasons to Helen.'

'I'm speaking on behalf of my colleagues, not *your* staff. Several of the surgeons have complained about working with nurses unused to their methods. And I agree with them.'

Abbey snapped, 'You seemed happy enough to work with a stranger when you tricked me into helping you.'

'What do you mean, "tricked"? And anyway, I've worked with you before. It wasn't a problem.'

'So I'll cancel the ad for bank staff?'

Max frowned and watched her with narrowed eyes. 'Just what are you trying to say?'

'If we enlarge the theatre bank it increases the possibility of you and all the other surgeons working with strangers.' She made the statement flatly, careful not to sound too triumphant.

'You're unreasonable, Abbey. Of course I don't want you to cancel it but I'm telling you, contract staff are what's needed. However, you've obviously made up your mind and nothing anyone can say is going to change it, so there's no point in wasting my breath.' He stood up. 'If you won't listen to advice, you'll never make a success of this place.'

'We'll see,' Abbey said quietly as he closed the door

behind him. Nevertheless, he left her tense and unable to relax until she made a conscious effort to do so. Annoyed with herself, she determined that she would ignore any future demands he might make, rather than waste valuable time spelling out the reason for her actions.

To her relief, Max and Helen left her in peace the next day and so by Friday, although tired, she was pleased with the progress she'd made.

She visited every department in the hospital that day and all the staff she met seemed to accept that, although she wasn't a pushover, she was prepared to listen and genuinely consider their requests which meant that she didn't find too many problems to deal with.

Her last visit was to the in-patients. As she approached the ward office, she saw Denny leaning on the doorjamb trying to distract the nurses from their work. 'What are you doing here?' she teased. 'I thought we'd seen the back of you once you were discharged.'

'I came for physio.'

'How's the knee?' Abbey asked.

'Fine. Well, not really. The physio thinks I'm not resting it enough. She was a bit worried about the wound today and thought one of the nurses ought to take a look, but they're awfully busy and Mum's waiting in the car park.'

'If it's just the wound you're worried about, I'll take a look for you.'

'Of course, you helped with the op so you'd know. Yeah, I'd like that.'

Abbey checked with the nurse in charge and took Denny to an empty room. She removed the dressing. 'Nothing wrong with the wounds that I can see, but it's quite swollen still. You're going to have rest it a lot more than you are doing.'

'That's what the physio said.'

'And I expect it'll be what Mr Darby would say as well. When are you seeing him again?'

'Monday.'

She replaced the support bandage and helped him from the bed. 'Well, if you don't want him to be angry at you spoiling his efforts, you'd better follow orders for the weekend.'

'I'll try. You won't tell him what it was like today, will you?'

Abbey agreed. 'But don't let me down, now.'

She returned to her office with mixed feelings. She had enjoyed her brief contact with the practical side of nursing, and wished there was some way she could combine more of it with the work she was now employed to do.

Discovering that Jane had already left for a well-earned weekend off, she decided to do the same, and so wasn't pleased when there was a peremptory pounding on her door.

Her heart sank even further when she saw it was Max. 'Yes?' she asked shortly, slipping on her jacket to make it clear that she was about to leave.

'Have you time for a quiet word, Abbey?' His dark eyes watched her closely.

Reluctantly she returned to her seat behind the desk. 'About what?'

'About standards and the amount of work we're continuing to lose to other hospitals.'

Unnerved by the note of query in his voice and the intensity of his gaze, Abbey looked down at her desk as she replied, 'The world's a competitive place, Max, in case you haven't noticed. But it's my problem, not yours.'

'Of course I've noticed. That's why I think we need an exchange of ideas.' He was becoming increasingly expansive. 'You see, I don't think it is entirely your problem. It's in the interests of all of us who work here that the hospital is a success.'

'Undoubtedly, but it's my place to worry about it. You have other concerns: your patients, your work elsewhere and especially keeping your skills up to date.'

'Are you implying that I don't?' he asked indignantly.

'No. Of course not. But putting things right is going to take more than a quiet word and—'

'That's why I'm here. I wondered if you were free for dinner tonight.'

'I'm afraid—'

'Tomorrow night, then?'

'I have to clear my old flat this weekend. I'll be too busy.'

'Perfect. We can talk as we work.'

'I don't need help, Max.' And I'm sure Helen wouldn't like it, she finished silently.

'I forgot you already have a resident helper.'

She shrugged noncommittally, but didn't attempt to tell him the truth.

'Surely he wouldn't object if I took you out to discuss this place over a meal?'

Abbey sighed deeply. 'I'm sorry, Max. I like to relax and get right away from the subject of work when I'm off duty.'

He shook his head ruefully. 'OK. If that's the way you feel, can I make an appointment for Monday instead?'

Abbey lifted her diary and nodded. 'I'm free around three. Is that any good?'

'Great. I should be able to manage that.'

'Three o'clock Monday, then.' She scribbled the time in her diary then made for the door.

'In the meantime, here's something to keep your mind busy over the weekend. If you're really serious about only taking on bank staff you're making a big mistake. If you don't increase the permanent theatre staff by the end of the month, I can tell you it'll be too late. Because there won't be many consultants left wanting to operate here. And I might not be one of them either.'

Abbey fumed as she made her way to the car park. If Max thought his threat would change her mind, he could think again. She would probably find her job much easier without him around! He obviously thought their previous acquaintance gave him the right to interfere. The sooner he accepted that it didn't, the better she would like it.

Despite a busy weekend spent rearranging her flat as she wanted it, Max was never far from her thoughts. She'd been too preoccupied at the time to wonder *why* he had so bitterly accused her of 'shacking up' with Ben. Because it had been over a month later that Ben's multiple sclerosis had taken a turn for the worse and she had offered to help her old schoolfriend by looking after him while Cheryl finished her law degree.

But, now she thought about it, Max had made it sound as if she'd disappeared the moment his back was turned. What—or who—had given him that idea she couldn't imagine. Nor why it should matter to him.

During their time together she'd believed that they had something special going, but when he hadn't bothered to get in touch she'd had to accept that he had seen it as nothing more than a casual fling. It had been a mark of her youthful gullibility that she'd ever thought otherwise.

On Sunday evening Cheryl brought Ben to see the flat.

'You've done wonders as usual, Abbey,' he told her, enunciating his words with difficulty.

'Coffee?' Abbey asked him. 'Or would you prefer something stronger to christen my new home?'

'Coffee, please.'

'Ben hardly ever touches alcohol these days, do you, love?' said Cheryl affectionately.

He shook his head in agreement and they both laughed at what Abbey presumed was a private joke.

'I expect you'd like to watch the end of the motor racing while I help with the drinks.' Cheryl switched on the television for him to watch and manoeuvred the wheelchair into a corner before following Abbey into the kitchen.

'I didn't say so in front of Ben but people can be so cruel. They see him in a wheelchair yet still think he speaks like that because he's been drinking. And it's getting worse rather than better.'

Abbey nodded. 'I know. It can't be easy for either of you. But don't forget, if there's ever anything I can do, anything at all—'

'We know. You've been far too good to us already. Mind you,' Cheryl teased, 'I wouldn't mind a little help with decorating. I don't know how you manage it—if I tried to put some of these colours together it would be a disaster.'

Abbey laughed. 'Perhaps you try too hard. I just don't think about it and it seems to work.'

'You ought to find yourself a husband.' Cheryl was suddenly serious. 'I don't believe you try. There must be hundreds of men out there searching for a skilled home-maker with your looks!'

'If that's all they're looking for, I'm content as I am,' Abbey retorted cheerfully. 'If, and it's a big if— if I marry, I want a relationship like yours and Ben's. You knew he had multiple sclerosis when you married him and that the prognosis wasn't good. But it made no difference. And I do believe that despite his present bad spell you're happier than you've ever been.'

Cheryl grinned engagingly. 'I think so too. I still go weak at the knees when he smiles. Have you never met anyone who made you feel that way?'

Abbey thought hard as she poured the boiling water into the cafetière, then said slowly, 'I did, once.'

Cheryl frowned. 'What happened?'

'He moved jobs and out of my life.' Abbey poured the coffee into the cups. 'I didn't hear from him again.'

'Didn't you try and contact him?'

'I didn't know where he was. He went off to do locum jobs and said he would contact me when he was settled, so when he didn't, I saw no point in trying to find him. If he'd been interested, he knew where I was. In many ways it suited me. It meant that I could concentrate on my career. Now, let's forget him and take this coffee through to Ben. He must wonder what we're doing.'

Cheryl ignored the suggestion and probed deeper. 'Perhaps your ambition frightened him away.'

Abbey laughed. 'I doubt it. I was a lowly scrub nurse at that time.'

'So, it must have been about the time of Ben's first relapse?'

'I suppose so.' Abbey lifted the tray and moved out of the kitchen. 'But let's not talk about him any more. He's past history.'

'Who's history?' Ben asked.

'Just a man—your wife is trying to discover why I'm not married.'

Ben took the cup of coffee she offered him. 'Cheryl wants everyone to be as happy as she is.'

'I am more than content with my lot. I love nursing and when I'm at home I like my own company.'

'And your new job?' Cheryl asked suspiciously.

Abbey was suddenly defensive. 'It'll be OK once I settle in.'

'You don't sound too sure.'

'It's different from anything I've done before. And I *was* warned that the medics don't take kindly to managers, but I'll show them.'

'The consultants ganging up on you, are they?' Cheryl laughed.

'No. Just the chairperson of the medical committee. An orthopod who thinks he knows better than me how to run the place. Almost threatening blackmail if I don't do as he thinks I should.'

'Blackmail?' Ben was horrified. 'Hey, that's serious.'

'Oh, nothing illegal. Just threatening not to bring any more work to the hospital and to take all the other consultants with him.'

'An orthopod?' Ben queried thoughtfully. 'Max Darby?'

Surprised, Abbey nodded. 'That's the one.'

'Max Darby,' Cheryl echoed. 'He's dishy.'

'How do you both know him?'

'You know Ben's dad is the chairman of the rugby club?' said Cheryl. 'Well, he has an arrangement with Max to deal with any injuries to the players.'

'I see.' Abbey uttered a silent prayer of thanks that she hadn't mentioned the name of the man to whom she had once given her heart.

'Surely the consultants would lose money as well if they all deserted the hospital?' Cheryl obviously thought that Abbey needed reassuring that Max wouldn't carry out his threat.

She shrugged. 'Course they would. That's why I've dismissed the threat as bravado. But it doesn't help having someone like that around when I'm trying to find my feet.'

'Just ignore him, Abbey. That's if you really want to, of course!'

Recognising that Cheryl was baiting her, Abbey grinned. 'I guess I'm just anticipating trouble that may never arise.'

Cheryl frowned. 'That's not a bit like you.'

'I've never been a hospital manager before.'

'Are you absolutely sure it's not your tall, handsome

adversary that's the problem?' Cheryl teased.

'He's certainly tall—in fact he's enormous; I'm dwarfed by him.'

Ben gave a shout of laughter. 'That's not difficult.'

'I don't know how we got into this conversation, especially as he already has a girlfriend.'

'Pity,' her friend laughed. 'I could see the film of the book! The surgeon and the new manager each working for the same end result, but unable to agree how to achieve it.'

'You're an incurable romantic, Cheryl.' Abbey sank onto her enormous bean bag. 'And always have been. I remember when we were at school—'

Cheryl raised her hands defensively. 'Don't give any of my secrets away.'

'All right. As long as you stop nagging me about my love life.'

'I promise. And am I going to be offered one of those scrumptious biscuits with my coffee?'

Abbey laughed and, proffering the plate, tried not to think about Max for the remainder of the evening.

However, she couldn't help remembering Cheryl's words when she was waiting for him to keep his appointment at three the next day. She'd been at her desk early and had worked without interruption throughout the morning, so she was confident that she now knew enough about the organisation of the hospital to discuss any suggestions knowledgeably.

He walked in without knocking and Abbey shook her head despairingly. 'If you don't report to Jane, she won't know you're here and we'll be disturbed.'

'And that might cause a scandal?' he asked provocatively.

Aware that her cheeks were flaming, Abbey snapped, 'Don't be so silly—'

'If it makes you feel better,' he interrupted quietly, 'I did report to Jane.'

'So why didn't she ring through to announce you?'

'I told her not to. Old friends like us don't need such formality. Don't you agree?'

'I'm glad to know we're still friends, but you must appreciate that the situation between us now is totally different.'

He grinned. 'You've made that very clear. Even so, I really do want to help you. That's why I suggested this chat. I thought it might clear the air between us.'

'Go ahead.'

'What do you think the main problem here is, then?'

Abbey shrank away from telling him. 'You tell me.'

'Lack of co-operation.'

'From who?'

'The previous managers. They have refused to listen to what anyone has to say. I was so sure *you* were going to be different.'

'Come off it, Max. I think we've known one another long enough to be honest.'

A knock on the door prevented him from replying, and Jane came in with a tray of tea.

'Thanks, Jane.' Abbey poured the tea as her secretary closed the door behind her. 'Sugar?'

He shook his head, pretending to be hurt. 'I thought you'd remember.'

Abbey handed him his cup and saucer. 'Don't you think rather too much water has gone under the bridge for that?'

He grinned shamelessly, his eyes searching her face relentlessly.

Embarrassed, she broke the silence by asking, 'Have you seen Denny Dale today? I wondered how he was progressing.'

Max checked his watch. 'I haven't forgotten your reason for taking on this job. I intend to let you know whether or not you participated in a successful operation. However, his appointment is not until five.'

Abbey felt her colour rising at his mockery. 'That wasn't the only reason.'

'Maybe not. So, after a week, what do *you* think the problem with this place is?'

Abbey had no hesitation in replying, 'You. And your colleagues. And the members of staff who see you as their champion.'

He frowned as he replaced his cup on the saucer. 'What, or who, are you talking about?'

'Don't come the old innocent with me. I'm well aware of the reason you are here.'

'And that is?' he asked, his voice suddenly so cold that Abbey was sure the temperature of the room had dropped.

'Helen has put you up to it. She thinks your support will add more weight to her demands and you've told her we're old friends and that you'll be able to talk me round.' She glared at him. 'I suppose you think I won't be able to resist it when you turn on the charm. Well, it's time you realised I've grown up. It must be quite a shock to you to find I'm no longer the little greenhorn you remember.'

She was pleased to note that she'd stopped him in his tracks. How dared he come here putting forward his girlfriend's proposals and pretending he was doing it because he wanted to help *her*, Abbey?

'You've got it all wrong, Abbey, but, if that's the way you see it, there's no point in discussing the matter further. Dear God, I said last week you'd become hard but I didn't realise how hard.'

Determined to keep up her advantage, Abbey asked, 'How's your brother-in-law, by the way? Recovering from his op OK?'

Annoyed at her reminding him of his deception, Max snapped, 'You know perfectly well he was fine when you checked up on him.'

Abbey was unsure whether she had scored a direct

hit or an own goal! 'If I didn't visit the patients and find out what they had to say, I wouldn't be doing my duty.'

'Hmm. You can't keep away from the nursing side, more like. I never saw your predecessors doing a ward round.'

'Perhaps that's why business is so bad?' Abbey countered quickly, to hide the fact that what he was saying was probably true.

'Rubbish—I've told you the reason for that already but you're determined not to listen. So it would be a waste of time and effort to repeat it.' He watched her silently for a few seconds, then asked quietly, 'Wouldn't it?'

The slow, seductive tone he used to ask the question made Abbey wonder if, after all, she was making a mistake. Perhaps he really did want to help.

When she didn't answer, he broke into her reverie abruptly. 'Changing the subject completely, Melissa has asked if you and your partner would like to join us for a thank-you meal this evening.'

'Melissa?' Her thoughts elsewhere, Abbey was unable for a minute to fit a face to the name.

Her expression must have mirrored her confusion because he swiftly added, 'My sister, remember? It's to say thank you for putting yourself out last Monday.'

'I see. It's very kind of her, but. . .' trying to hide her surprise, Abbey sought an excuse '. . .Ben's away for a few days.'

Even if he wasn't her 'partner', that bit at least was the truth. Cheryl had taken him into the neuro hospital that morning for reassessment.

'In that case come alone. I could collect you. Mel's house isn't easy to find in the dark.'

Abbey was torn. Her heart was urging her to say yes, while her head warned that it would be a dangerous thing to do. Eventually, ignoring the logic of her mind, she decided it could do no harm. After all, they had to work together whether she liked it or not and she couldn't keep on making excuses to Melissa. If she was ready early she could meet him on the doorstep. 'OK. I'll give you the address of my flat.' She scribbled hurriedly. 'It's just at the end of the airport perimeter on Woolley Road.'

Max's hand brushed hers as he took the paper and he scrutinised her features closely until she averted her gaze. He read the address and nodded. 'I know the place. I'll be there about a quarter to eight.'

Wondering if Helen was also invited, she watched him close the door. Hopefully, if nothing else, the evening would raise their working relationship onto a more amicable footing, free of inhibiting memories from the past.

CHAPTER THREE

As SHE was leaving the hospital later that afternoon, Abbey bumped into Denny Dale.

'Hi, Denny, how's the knee today?'

'Much better. I've just seen Mr Darby and he's very pleased. Good job he didn't see it on Friday, eh? I've tried to keep off it all weekend, like you said.'

'I'm pleased to hear it.' His infectious good humour transferred itself to Abbey, and as she drove home she began to look forward to the evening out.

It was a good job she intended to be ready early. She wasted far too much time rummaging through her wardrobe, hoping for miracles, but nothing she tried on looked right for the occasion. She finally settled on the faithful black silk dress that seemed suitable for any occasion.

However, thwarting all her plans not to invite him in, it was barely half past seven when she answered the peal of the doorbell and found Max standing there.

Barefoot and without make-up, she felt naked as he surveyed her from head to toe. Moving closer, he gently grasped her upper arms and greeted her with a light kiss on the cheek. 'You look more like a vivacious teenager than a hospital manager. *I* wouldn't leave such a prize for a moment, let alone for a night!'

His eyes glinted dangerously as Abbey pulled away from him, trying desperately to hide the traitorous pleasure she felt at his compliment.

Despite the insistent thought that he had left her alone for a lot longer than that, she was suddenly unsure of herself.

She asked nervously, 'Is—wouldn't Helen like to come in for a moment as well?'

'Helen?' he queried with a frown. 'She's not with me. Why should she be?'

Her heart gave an unconscious flip at his denial. 'I—I just presumed she'd be going as well.'

'Why?'

'I—I—no reason,' Abbey stuttered. The sooner she escaped from this crazy conversation the better. 'Would you like a drink while you're waiting?'

Max shook his head. 'Not at the moment, thanks. I would like to know, though, what you mean by conspiring with my patients behind my back.'

Abbey thought she detected a glint of humour in his eyes, but she wasn't sure. 'What do you mean, your patients?'

'One Denny Dale, to be exact. Told him to take it easy before I saw it or I'd hit the roof.'

Abbey was abject. 'Is that what he told you? I didn't mean it that way. I—I—.'

He laughed as she floundered, lost for words. 'I'm very grateful to you.' He took hold of both her hands and pulled her towards him. 'I would have been furious if he'd undone all my good work.'

'I do do the right thing occasionally, then?' she retorted sharply.

He looked surprised by her response. 'You would have known in the old days that I was only teasing.' His voice was gentle but the heat of his gaze hinted at an intimacy that no longer existed.

She pulled her hands free and, determined to escape the tension building between them, pushed open the door to her sitting room.

'Come through and sit down.'

He did as she asked, but not before she'd noted the despairing shake of his head at her rebuff. He looked around the room with admiration. 'Nice decor.'

'All my own work. I did it before I moved in,' she told him proudly before realising her mistake.

He gave a wry grin as he shook his head slowly, and she knew he hadn't missed her admission that she was living there alone. However, he didn't question it. 'It's incredible the way those colours mingle to make the room seem so large.'

'I'm glad you like it. I once considered going in for interior design but decided to stick with my first ambition.'

'Which is?'

'To get to a position where I can influence the course of future health care. Over the years I've become increasingly disillusioned with the present set-up. I suppose that sounds pompous to you but—'

'Not at all,' he reassured her, 'but I don't understand how you intend to do it from a small private hospital. You should be in the thick of things.'

'I'm aware of that,' Abbey told him huffily, 'but I had to start somewhere. Management jobs are not exactly two-a-penny these days.'

'No,' he conceded thoughtfully. 'I think I begin to understand.'

'You do?'

'I remember you once telling me that you'd gone with your mother to visit your father in hospital and you'd both been appalled by the lack of properly trained staff. Is that the reason for your decision?'

'Partly.' Afraid that the colour flooding her cheeks would tell him that it wasn't the whole truth, she rushed on, 'And partly because I can see it getting worse. All this talk of de-skilling means the trained nurses are locked away doing paperwork while patients are looked after by caring people, but people who would never recognise an important change in a patient's condition in a month of Sundays.'

Max was grinning at her, with eyebrows raised.

'I see. So, what about the paperwork you're languishing under?'

'OK. You can mock me. But you did ask. Anyway, enough about work. I'd better jump off my soapbox and apply a few finishing touches. Won't be a moment.' Already regretting her outburst, she added. 'Take a seat. The evening paper's there if you'd like it.'

She ran into her bedroom and, having closed the door, put on her tights and made up her face, wondering all the time just what he wanted from her. Was he merely trying to manipulate her into agreeing to his way of doing things at the hospital, or was he hoping to resurrect their earlier liaison? And, if so, on what basis? Temporary or permanent?

Was that why Helen wasn't joining them? Unable to come to any conclusion, she slipped on a pair of black strappy sandals and made her way back to the sitting room.

'That was quick.' He helped her into the black jacket she was holding.

As he assisted her into the passenger seat of the dark blue BMW she thought of Helen leaving the hospital in the same seat and wondered if he'd told her about this evening's meal. Deciding that it was none of her business, she settled back to enjoy the outing—whatever his reasons for asking her.

'I do agree with you, you know.'

Guessing that he could only be referring to her earlier outburst, Abbey prompted, 'But?'

'How did you know I was going to qualify my agreement?'

She grinned nervously. 'From your tone of voice. It's OK. I know I'm a throwback from the past, and—'

'Don't put yourself down. My reservation was merely financial. Professional staff cost money, as you're already discovering.'

Abbey nodded. 'There must be a better way, though.'

'I hope you find it. I really do. For all our sakes.' He brought the car to a standstill in the drive of a modern, detached house already boasting two cars.

As she climbed from the BMW the security light came on, allowing Abbey to see that the house was older—and larger—than she had first thought.

'Come and meet the family.' He grasped her arm as he pushed open the unlocked door. 'You'll enjoy this. Melissa's a fantastic cook.'

'Have they any children?'

'Two—a boy and a girl—but they won't be here tonight. They are boarders from Monday to Friday.'

'Is the school too far away to travel to daily?'

'Oh, no. They go to Bleasdon Grammar. It just means they can take more part in the after-school activities. They get the best of both worlds that way.'

'I see.'

Abbey allowed herself to be propelled inside and smiled warmly when Melissa came to greet her. 'Good to see you—er—Miss Westray?'

'Do call me Abbey. Thanks for inviting me.'

'We wanted to thank you for putting yourself out for Peter. I don't know how Max managed to talk you into it, but we're so grateful he did. It means Pete should be fit and well for our late skiing holiday. We're going to Canada this year.'

So that was why Max had applied the pressure! Not to save the business but to save his sister's holiday. Abbey felt the heat flood to her cheeks at the thought of him duping her. What was the matter with her that her normally infallible perception seemed to desert her where Max was concerned?

Relieved that the comfortable seat she had taken was near enough to the roaring log fire to explain her high colour, she turned to Peter and asked, 'How are you feeling?'

'Fine. I can't believe how well. I certainly can't complain about any part of my treatment at St Luke's.'

'I'm pleased to hear it.' Abbey's smile was warm until she added drily, 'Max isn't quite so complimentary about the place.'

'That's a bit unfair,' Max protested. 'I'm only trying to point you in the right direction until you find your feet. As chairman of the MedCom, I feel it's my duty.'

'Time to come and eat.' Melissa appeared from the direction of the kitchen, preventing Abbey from voicing her scepticism.

When they were all seated, and Abbey had congratulated their hostess on the excellent avocado and prawn mousse with which they were starting the meal, Melissa said to Abbey, 'I gather you and Max have worked together before?'

She nodded. 'Quite a long time ago.'

'So you didn't know he was working at St Luke's?'

'His name was mentioned amongst others at my interview, but I didn't expect to be working closely with him. It was quite a surprise when I found he was the new chairperson.'

'A pleasant one, I hope?' Max's eyes gleamed as he raised his glass of red wine tauntingly to his lips.

When Abbey didn't immediately answer, he replaced his drink on the table and said challengingly, 'Obviously not!'

Abbey protested. 'Of course it was a pleasant surprise. It's always nice to meet up with old colleagues.'

'I see,' Max replied thoughtfully, watching her closely.

His scrutiny made her uncomfortable. She wished she'd never agreed to come. His behaviour was confirming her suspicion that this was no thank-you meal, but that he'd engineered the invitation.

He was making it clear that if neither sweet talk nor threats achieved the results he sought he was ready to try other methods.

Peter appeared to sense the tension between them and changed the subject. 'Have you any holiday plans for this year, Abbey?'

She shook her head. 'As I hoped to be starting a new job, I thought I'd wait before settling on any dates.'

'Are you a skier?' Max asked.

Abbey laughed ruefully. 'Not really. I spent one holiday with a group of nurses on the Italian slopes, but I don't think that qualifies me to claim to be a skier.'

'Did you enjoy it?' Max asked.

'It was great. Once I'm settled in here I might consider doing it again.'

'Did you know there's a dry ski slope opened up locally?'

Abbey nodded. 'I had heard. But I'm not sure I'm interested. There was one near an accident and emergency department where I once worked and they seemed to produce far more injuries than occur on the snow.'

'I haven't heard of any problems at this one. You should try it one day.'

'When work permits,' Abbey joked. 'Which hopefully shouldn't be for some time yet. I prefer to keep my limbs out of the hands of you orthopods.'

'All work and no play?' Max teased, inclining his head. 'You know what they say.'

Abbey ignored the taunt and asked Melissa, 'Do the children go with you?'

She nodded, 'That's why we go so late—we have to wait for the school holidays.'

'I see. I expect that's the best age to learn.'

'Mel and I learnt to ski the moment we could stand—*that's* the very best time of all. We're both experts, aren't we, Sis?'

Melissa laughed. 'You might be. I'm certainly not.'

'Very nice, if you have the opportunity,' Abbey responded drily. 'Few of us do, though.'

Melissa laughed again. 'We only had the chance because Dad was posted to Canada! Take no notice of Max. He's winding you up.'

Something he's been doing since the moment I met up with him again, Abbey thought angrily as Melissa brought the main course through. Why, oh, why did he have to become the MedCom chairman at this most inconvenient of times?

Realising that she would not find an answer to that, she made up her mind to ignore his attempts to unsettle her and enjoy the spread being laid before them. Melissa carved the glistening rack of lamb and Abbey helped herself to a wide array of vegetables.

'This is superb, Melissa,' she complimented her after tasting her first mouthful.

'We've all been given different talents, you for nursing—and interior design, Melissa for preparing fantastic meals, Pete for figures and me for needlework.'

'Needlework?' Abbey queried, then, seeing the laughter in his eyes, realised he was talking about suturing wounds.

'We should use the skills we've got instead of trying to be what we're not,' Max told her archly.

Aware that his amusement was meant to disguise another criticism of her move to management, she said, 'But if we don't try we'll never know what other talents we have.'

'Touché.' He again raised his glass to his lips, the laughter in his eyes spilling over onto his face.

Embarrassed by the obvious intimacy he was trying to suggest, Abbey refused to meet his gaze throughout the remainder of the meal.

When it was time to take their leave she thanked

Melissa warmly. 'I haven't had such an enjoyable evening for a long time. Thanks again.'

On the way home she felt Max give her several quick glances before he said, 'When are you going to relax?'

She was indignant. 'What do you mean?'

'You've been like a coiled spring all evening.'

'What do you expect when all that rot you've been feeding me for the past week or so about saving the business was for no other reason than so your sister could have her skiing holiday?'

'It wasn't only that, Abbey,' he told her quietly. 'All right, I know I should have told you who the patient was, but I didn't want to complicate matters. Whatever you might think, my main reason was to prevent Tom changing his allegiance.'

'Humph.'

'You can disagree all you like, but I know what the Cotswold is offering because I've been approached as well.'

Abbey bridled. 'I've told you before—it's my problem. I'm already trying to do something about it, and I can assure you that I do not respond to blackmail.'

'Blackmail? What blackmail?'

'Your threats to move elsewhere and take the other consultants with you.'

'That certainly wasn't blackmail. Every word was the truth. However, if you don't want to believe it, I promise I won't mention it again. I also promise that I'll say "I told you so" if you ignore my warning and things go from bad to worse.'

She sighed deeply. 'I appreciate your concern, Max, but I won't be stampeded into inappropriate action because you, or any of the other consultants, think that's the way we need to go. When I came for my interview the group manager warned against just that.'

'Abbey, they've appointed you to change the fortunes of this place. They should let you get on with it in your own way. We're only the second hospital in the group and it's taken all this time to get the first one financially sound. So I don't think you could exactly call them experts, and if this place fails the company will go under. Then you'll be out of a job with a reputation for failure to live down. It's in your own interests to act fast.'

Her answering retort was drowned by the urgent summons of his mobile phone. 'Max Darby speaking.' He listened intently. 'Yes. Yes. I understand.'

Abbey could just make out a female voice at the other end of the line, but not what was being said.

When it stopped speaking he asked, 'And what happened when you did that?'

He was given more information. 'I'd better come over and see for myself.' He closed down the telephone. 'It's your RMO. Saturday's fractured femur is giving cause for concern. Do you mind if we call at the hospital before I drop you home?'

'Not at all. If I can do anything to help. . .' Her voice tailed off as she realised that he was deep in thought.

As they climbed from his car at the hospital door, she murmured, 'Give me a call if you need me.'

'Aren't you coming up to the ward with me?'

'I—er—I wasn't. Do you want me to?'

'Of course—I may need to take Mrs Jenkins to Theatre again.'

Recognising his meaning, Abbey argued gently as they waited for the lift, 'There are theatre staff on call—'

'And you're on the spot. You wouldn't refuse to help, would you?'

Aware that he was thinking only of the patient, she could do nothing but agree. 'Well, no, I suppose not, but it's not going to look good to my staff, us arriving together.'

'I'll make sure they all know I received the call at
an official function and asked you to come with me.'
He sounded exasperated by her fears, so she refrained
from arguing further.

Mrs Jenkins was resting comfortably when they
entered her room.

'What have you been up to?' Max teased her
gently.

The patient shook her head wearily. 'The nurses
keep disturbing me to change the dressing.'

The senior night nurse joined them at that moment
and after Abbey introduced herself explained, 'There's
a fair amount of discharge from her wound when she
moves about.'

'Infection?' asked Abbey sharply, her immediate
concern reflecting her theatre training.

'No, just a leakage of serous fluid, but the RMO
was a little worried that, with her poor condition, it
could indicate that the wound is opening up.'

'Is her blood pressure OK?' Max asked, lifting the
charts.

The nurse shrugged. 'It's difficult to gauge. As you
know, it's been pretty low since the accident.'

'Let's have a look at the site.' Max stood back to
allow Abbey to uncover the operation site while the
nurse went for a dressing pack.

Max frowned as he examined the area. 'It doesn't
look to be opening up,' he murmured to Abbey. 'But
I'm not sure what's happening here. I'll go and have
a word with Ellie.'

Abbey helped the night nurse to re-dress the wound
and make Mrs Jenkins comfortable.

She found Max in the ward office, writing up his
findings. He was slumped in an armchair and she
thought how tired he looked. She waited anxiously to
see what decision he'd come to.

Eventually he looked up and smiled at her. 'I've had

a word with Ellie and I'm almost certain it's not a major problem, but we need to keep an eye on her just in case. She's a poor old thing so I'm reluctant to take her back to Theatre unless it's an absolute necessity.

'However, if we stop her moving around altogether it increases the danger of deep vein thrombosis so I've suggested just curtailing her movements for the next twenty-four hours and have slightly increased her anti-coagulants.' He wrote a few comments in the patient's notes. 'I'll be in first thing in the morning to see her anyway. Come on, let's get out of here while the going's good.'

As they went down in the lift Abbey offered to get a taxi home. 'You need your sleep if you're going to be back here early in the morning,' she added.

'It won't take a moment to drop you home. I'm not in the habit of shirking my responsibilities.' The lift doors opened and, nodding to the night porter, he strode out of the building, making it difficult for her to keep up.

His responsibility! He made her sound like a box of groceries! As he unlocked his car she protested fiercely, 'I'm quite capable of making my own way home, Max.'

'Well, you're not going to. Stop arguing and get in.'

Abbey reluctantly did so, but remained uncommunicative throughout the short journey.

When he pulled up outside her flat he turned her face towards him with a gentle touch and, before she could protest, brushed her lips with his. 'Good to be working with you again, Abbey. I'm sorry we didn't manage the tête-à-tête I had planned to round off a pleasant evening. Perhaps we could try again later in the week?'

His kiss had awoken a flurry of sensations that, until that moment, Abbey had hoped were buried too deep to resurrect. Unable to trust herself, she stammered, 'I—I'm not sure. Th—thanks for the lift.' She struggled to open the passenger door.

Max reached across to prevent her. 'Goodnight, Abbey, I'll no doubt see you tomorrow.'

Sensing a proprietorial confidence, she pulled away from him sharply. 'Thanks for the lift home. And Max—' he looked at her hopefully '—do thank your sister again for the lovely meal.'

She sensed his disappointment and wondered if he had thought she was about to offer him coffee. If so, he was out of luck. She had no intention of entering into another casual affair just because they'd been thrown together by a whim of fate. However attractive she might still find him.

Nevertheless, she was in to work early the next morning, hoping that Max would let her know what was happening to Mrs Jenkins before he set about his day's routine.

When she had heard nothing by ten she asked Penny, who had arrived to discuss her budget.

'Everything seems to have settled today. She's back to mobilising normally.'

Abbey received the news with mixed feelings. She was happy to know that the patient didn't need further surgery, but she was disappointed that Max hadn't bothered to let her know after her help the previous evening.

Pushing all thoughts of him from her mind, she concentrated for the next hour on discussing with Penny ways of attracting more business.

'Do you think a couple of open days might attract more patients to the hospital?' Abbey asked. 'Once they've seen what we have to offer, they might bring pressure on the consultants to be treated here rather than anywhere else.'

'Sounds like a good idea. People I speak to outside

the profession really don't know what we do here.'

'Right. I'll get down to arranging an open day or two and publicising them. In the meantime, if you have any other ideas let me know.'

When Penny left, Abbey found Helen waiting to see her. 'Max tried to have a word with you but you were busy and he couldn't wait. He's asked me to pass on some information.'

'Yes?' Abbey was irritated at his using Helen as his messenger.

'A couple of our surgeons have decided to admit their patients to the Cotswold. Mr Brewton the urologist and Mr Inklin.'

Abbey frowned. 'The gynae man? Why?'

'I couldn't fit in lists at the times they wanted and, having heard you'd helped out with Max's brother-in-law, it didn't go down at all well. They thought you should do the same for them.'

'Why on earth did Max get involved?'

'He was in the hospital when they started creating, so I asked him to come down.' She must have read the anger on Abbey's face as she rushed to defend her action. 'He *is* chairman of the MedCom.'

'All right.' Abbey recognised that there was no point in berating Helen. The incident had Max's hallmark written all over it. 'I'll try and see them both as soon as possible. I've had time now to assess the ward situation and it seems they can cope for the moment with an increase in day cases, but anything more will cause a problem.'

'I suppose that's a start, but we can't make any plans until we see what the response is to the ad. Nothing so far, I suppose?'

'No, but it only went off on Friday. It hasn't appeared in the paper as yet. Look, Helen, I'm sorry you've had this unpleasantness, but if anything like this should arise again please let me know. Immediately. Under those circumstances I don't mind being disturbed, whoever I'm with.'

Helen's mutinous expression made it clear to Abbey that she would do exactly the same again if Max wanted her to.

'Was there anything else?' she asked dismissively, knowing that, under the circumstances, trying to get a promise from Helen about any future action would be an impossibility.

Helen shook her head. 'I'm scrubbing for the ENT list at eleven-thirty, so I'll have to go.'

Abbey watched her leave with some misgivings. There was little she could do except ask Jane to contact the two surgeons Helen had mentioned and invite them to come and see her. Whether they would was out of her hands.

She settled down to further study of the budget plans and worked through her lunch break. By three she thought she could see a way of paying for extra permanent staff in both Theatre and the wards, providing that the number of cases they treated fell no further. So it was imperative that she persuade these two renegades back into the fold. She would have to make it clear to Helen that her allegiance should be to the hospital manager rather than to the consultants.

Jane came in at that moment. 'You're summoned to a chat with the Group bigwigs at the Mercy next week. They want the chairman of the MedCom as well.'

Abbey had been told at her interview that she would have a chance to see how the sister hospital was managed, but she hadn't expected to have to take Max with her or meet the company managers at such an early stage.

'Is that normal? I mean the invitation to Mr Darby.'

'Oh, yes. Mr Glennie often went with the previous

manager, although I can't say they were ever impressed with what they saw.'

'Which day do they want us to go?'

'They've left that up to you.'

Abbey shrugged. 'It'll depend on Mr Darby's other commitments if they want him as well, though for the life of me I can't see why it's necessary.'

'Would you like me to contact his secretary and see what she says? He might not have time to go with you.'

Hoping that that would turn out to be the case, Abbey nodded eagerly. 'That'd be great, Jane.'

Jane came back to Abbey later. 'Mr Darby is free on Friday afternoon next week.'

Abbey consulted her diary and sighed. 'It looks as if that's OK by me as well, so, providing it suits the powers that be, you'd better book it.'

She had just returned to her paperwork when the telephone rang. 'Can you come to the ward, Miss Westray?' It was Penny. 'As soon as you can, please.'

What now? 'I'll come straight down.'

As she ran down the stairs she began to wonder just what she'd let herself in for when she'd taken this job. She'd wanted a challenge and it certainly seemed that she was getting one.

Neither the theatre sister nor the ward sister appeared prepared to take the responsibility she considered they were paid for. Instead they were using her as an old-style matron, rather than a hospital manager. She couldn't believe they'd been the same with the previous managers, both male and neither of whom had had nursing experience. Perhaps it was because she'd assisted Max with a theatre case on her first day? If so, she was experiencing repercussions from the action that she hadn't thought about when she agreed to do it.

Penny met her at the foot of the stairs and anxiously

led the way into the ward office and closed the door.

'Problem, I'm afraid.'

'What?' Abbey asked fearfully.

'One of Mr Renny's patients collapsed following his return from Theatre to close his colostomy opening. He wasn't found until it was time for the fifteen-minute check on his pulse and blood pressure.'

Abbey forced herself to remain calm. 'How is he now?'

'Stable. We've got him under constant observation and thank goodness there doesn't seem to be any permanent damage.'

Abbey let out the breath she'd been unconsciously holding. 'How did it happen?'

'We can't watch them every minute when they're in thirty separate rooms,' Penny said, defending her staff loyally.

'I appreciate that. Has Mr Renny seen him?'

'No, only the RMO and the anaesthetist.'

'But Mr Renny's been informed?'

Penny assured her that he had. 'He'd already left the building when it happened, but he says he'll be back to see him later.'

'Well, I can't seen that we can do anything else at the moment. Fill in an incident form and keep me informed about the patient's progress. Mr Tate, isn't it? Everything went well when they closed the abdominal opening, did it?'

'Yes. In fact Mr Renny thought it so successful that he expected the bowel to function normally sooner than usual.'

Abbey nodded. 'I'll go and see him now.'

The patient was resting quietly so she nodded a greeting to the nurse seated at his bedside and, after checking the various charts, asked quietly, 'Any problems?'

The girl shook her head. 'His heart was fibrillating.

The beat stabilised after a couple of shocks from the machine. By that time the entire crash team had arrived with an anaesthetist. He took control and everything ran very smoothly.'

'It's good to know the cardiac arrest system works so efficently.'

'We were lucky that the anaesthetist was still in the hospital.'

Abbey nodded, pleased by the rapid response of the team.

She was reluctant to leave the premises until she knew the outcome, so she was still there at seven when Max came in search of her.

'I suppose you've heard what happened today?'

Abbey counted to ten. 'If you mean Mr Renny's patient, yes, I have heard.'

'I suppose you realise that this is all down to bad management. If Mr Tate hadn't pulled through, his death would have been laid at your door.'

CHAPTER FOUR

'I REALISE nothing of the sort, Max. This is something that can happen at any time when patients are nursed in single rooms.'

'Come off it, Abbey. You know as well as I do that post-operative patients should have constant supervision.'

'Don't be so unreasonable, Max,' she told him quietly. 'Patients are not allowed out of the recovery suite until they're considered to be in no danger. And yet when they arrive back on the ward they are monitored every quarter of an hour for much longer than necessary. Look at the pulse and blood-pressure charts of your patients if you don't believe me. If the checks hadn't been done, Mr Renny's patient might not have been found as soon as he was.'

'That's not—'

Abbey interrupted forcefully, 'However, I am glad you've raised the subject. Perhaps now you can understand why I can't increase the number of operations without increasing the numbers of staff on the ward.'

He didn't answer, but asked instead, 'Why the summons to the Mercy? Why do we both need to go?'

Aware that for once she had the upper hand on the subject of staffing, she hid a smile as she replied, 'At the interview they said I would have a chance to go and see how it's run. They obviously think it would be better if you understood what we're trying to achieve at St Luke's as well.'

'Ridiculous. I can't see any need for that! And do I have to see the bigwigs as well?'

'I certainly hope so,' she told him with a twinkle in

her eye. 'Should be quite an experience. Head Office is apparently sited in a swish old house in the Mercy grounds. Jane says Mr Glennie went over there several times and said it had to be seen to be believed.'

'I'd better have a word with him. See what it's all about.' He regarded her steadily for a few moments. 'Now, tell me why you're still here at this time of night?'

Unwilling to meet his gaze, Abbey looked down at the papers on her desk. 'I'm waiting to hear what Tom has to say about his patient. He hasn't been in yet.'

'He arrived as I came up here.'

'I'll contact the ward in a minute and see what's happening. In the meantime—' she returned to the offensive '—what about these two surgeons who I'm told have taken their business elsewhere? It wasn't your place to deal with the problem. If you'd rung Jane she would have let me know the situation and I could have sorted it out there and then. As it is, I'm not finding it easy to arrange a meeting with either of them.'

As she harangued him she thought she detected a sheepish look cross his face, causing her to wonder if the message could possibly have been in retaliation for her not inviting him in for coffee the previous evening. 'Their secretaries don't seem to know what Jane's talking about,' she told him suspiciously. 'That message you sent with Helen *was* genuine, was it?'

'Well, perhaps not exactly, but they were both fuming and it took me a long time to calm them down. If they do come back here, it'll only be because they recognise the facilities are so much better. And if they still can't operate when they want to they won't stay.'

'And you consider yourself the right person to calm them down?' she asked sarcastically. 'When it was your trickery on my first day that made them think exceptions can be made?'

'That's unfair, Abbey. Don't try and put the blame onto me. It may have been my brother-in-law who needed the surgery, but it served to prove a point.'

The telephone rang and, lifting the receiver, Abbey heard the voice of the senior nurse telling her that Mr Renny was satisfied with his patient's condition.

'Right, I'll be down to see him in a moment.' She finished the call and rose from her chair, indicating that their chat was over.

Max opened the door for her. 'When you've finished there, how about a bite to eat?'

As she raised her eyes to search his face, the look she read in his eyes spelt out the danger of accepting. 'I'm afraid I can't.' She had recognised the previous evening that the only way to prevent further damage to her emotions was to limit their time together. 'I've had a busy day and there are still things I must do. Especially as we were out so late last night.' Their respective positions might mean that she couldn't avoid him altogether but she had no intention of meeting up with him more than was absolutely necessary.

'We needn't take long—it'll be quicker than cooking for yourself. And that's what you would be doing, isn't it?'

She ignored his clumsy attempt to discover if, and why, she lived alone. 'I'd rather not, thanks all the same, Max.'

Shrugging, he grinned ruefully. 'Age must have robbed me of some of my charm. You never refused an invitation to eat in the past—'

'Max, I keep telling you—'

'I know. You're a different person these days. OK. I'll back off and leave you to your solitude. Because that's what you're returning to, isn't it? An empty flat?'

Abbey toyed with the idea of denying it, but decided that the only way she could keep their relationship a working one was to give him as little information as possible. 'I don't think that's any concern of yours.'

He shook his head disbelievingly, then, shrugging, muttered, 'Point taken, I suppose.'

Abbey was thoughtful as she watched him stride down the corridor. She recalled his comment on her first day in the post that she had 'shacked up' with someone else the moment his back was turned. If he really believed that, and was not just excusing his own behaviour, she supposed she ought to set the record straight.

And yet all the time he thought there was another man in her life she could keep him where she wanted him—as far removed from her susceptibility as possible.

She locked her office and made her way to the ward. Finding Mr Tate's condition stable, she had a quick word with Tom Renny. 'Everything all right?'

Tom nodded. 'He's doing well now. I've no worries about him. Your staff were certainly on the ball.'

Encouraged by his comments, Abbey smiled. 'Good. Nursing the patients in separate rooms does have its problems, but the nurses cope very well.'

'I certainly have no complaints.'

She passed on Tom Renny's compliment to the nursing staff, then, before heading for home, went to make one last check on Mr Tate.

She was surprised to find no one in the room with him, and when she saw him slumped across the bed, the drip tube pulled so tight that she was sure the needle must be out of his arm, she couldn't believe her eyes. She raced across to him, pressing the nurse call button on the way. He looked up at her with vacant eyes. 'I wanted the bathroom.'

Two nurses had answered her call by that time and she heard one gasp, 'I only left him to get a bottle.'

Together the three of them moved him into bed and the nurse looking after him examined the site of entry of the intravenous drip and checked his operation site.

By some miracle the needle was still in place and there was no apparent damage to his wound. The other nurse handed Mr Tate the bottle to use and they all withdrew to give him privacy.

'How long were you away?' Abbey asked.

'A minute at the most. He was fidgety and said he wanted to go to the toilet so I told him what I was doing and rushed to get the receptacle.' The young nurse was obviously terrified by what had occurred. 'I can't believe he could move so quickly.'

'You should know better than to leave a patient in his condition for even a second,' Abbey cautioned sharply. 'If you need anything else, for goodness' sake, call another nurse.'

She left, confident that the young nurse had learnt a lesson she wouldn't forget.

Nevertheless, she made her way to the ward office and asked the senior nurse to make a complete note of all that had happened, both on an incident form and in the patient's notes.

She had intended to go straight to Cheryl's flat and find out what was happening with Ben, but after the day she'd had, and the delay while she'd waited for news of Mr Tate, she was too tired to even think about it. She hoped Cheryl would not object if tonight she just telephoned.

It was the first thing she did when she got home, just in case Cheryl needed her physical presence.

'Hi. It's Abbey. How's things?'

'OK, I suppose.'

'What's the matter?'

Cheryl didn't answer immediately. 'I'm not used to being here on my own. I miss Ben dreadfully. And now they're talking about keeping him in for several days while they start trials of a new treatment.'

'What's that?'

'Don't know any details. I'm not sure we will, either. Sounds like it'll be what they call a blind trial. Some will get the drug and some a harmless pill. We won't know until the end which one he's taking.'

'How does Ben feel about it?'

'Oh, you know him. Willing to try anything. He can't wait. But enough about us. How's your day been? Gone any more rounds with your troublesome consultant?'

Abbey laughed. 'Not exactly. But he's wearing me out with his attempts to get the better of me. I'm all in this evening.'

'Come for a meal tomorrow evening, then we can have a good gossip.'

'I'd like that, thanks, Cheryl. Are you sure you're OK there on your own?'

Cheryl laughed at the other end of the line. 'Of course I am. I was just feeling sorry for myself when you rang.'

'OK. If you're sure. Give my love to Ben when you see him.'

'Will do. And Abbey, thanks for calling. See you tomorrow.'

She ended the call and Abbey slumped thankfully into an easy chair.

Anxiety about Mr Tate's condition meant that Abbey was in the hospital much earlier than usual the following morning. She went straight up to the ward to check on him.

'He's doing fine,' the night sister told her. 'No problem.' She led the way into the patient's room and told Mr Tate who Abbey was.

He looked up at her with a toothless grin. 'Scared the lot of you, didn't I?'

'You did rather,' Abbey told him, 'but I'm glad to see you're none the worse for it.'

'Tough old horse, I am. And your gals have been wonderful—they haven't left me alone for a moment.'

Abbey grinned at the description of her nurses. 'I'm pleased to hear it. Now don't overdo things today, will you?'

'Not much chance of that, attached to this.' He indicated the drip feeding into a vein in his arm. 'Sooner I can tuck into a rare steak the better.'

'You'll have to wait a few days for that. It'll take time to get your gut working properly again. You don't look very comfortable slumped down in the bed like that. Let's try and do something about it.'

As they finished, the nurse was called away. Mr Tate told Abbey, 'That's much better. You ought to be a nurse as well!'

Abbey laughed with him but, noting his exhaustion, didn't attempt to explain and left him, promising to look in and see him the next day.

Max was walking down the corridor when she emerged. With a teasing glint in his eye, he enquired, 'Guilty conscience after all?'

Abbey glared at him. 'Certainly not!'

'We don't often see management in at this hour of the day. Didn't even think you knew it existed.'

She didn't rise to the taunt. Instead she countered, 'I consider my staff deserve my appreciation and support, especially at difficult times. Now, if you'll excuse me, I have work to do even if you don't.'

'Oh, but I do. I've just seen one of your greatest fans and told him he should be able to go home tomorrow.' At Abbey's puzzled frown, he added, 'Mr Murray.'

'The hip replacement? I haven't had a lot to do with him.'

'No? You obviously made an impression on him. He tells me a manager with nursing experience is a good thing.'

'Which you don't agree with.'

'I have never said that. All I said was I didn't think it was the job for you. And I still don't.'

'Too bad,' she responded tartly. 'Because I'm here now and enjoying every minute of it.'

As she turned towards the stairwell, she saw his eyebrows raised in disbelief.

However, he appeared to dog her every footstep for the next twenty-four hours and each time they met up his complaints became progressively more spurious.

Thursday afternoon was the limit as far as Abbey was concerned. He stormed angrily into her office. 'Do you know that last night my clinic time was cut short because a psychologist needed the consulting room, and, on top of that, when Jack Kirklan wanted to book an ENT case into Theatre there was no one around who knew what they were doing?'

Abbey didn't answer, but leaned back in her chair and shook her head.

'Well, what are you going to do about it?'

'Nothing.'

'Nothing?' Max repeated explosively.

'You consultants have been spoilt ever since you came to work here. If you check the terms of your contract you will see that the consulting rooms are let out to you on a sessional basis and, out of the kindness of our heart, we've allowed you to run over into the next session when no one required the room.

'Having now attracted new business to the hospital, we are going to have to limit you all to your contracted hours.'

'New business?' he queried scathingly. 'It's not the sort of business that will bring the in-patients you need.'

'Maybe not, but every little helps.'

Increasingly infuriated, he demanded, 'So what about the theatre bookings?'

'What about them? I can't pay someone to sit there twenty-four hours a day just so that you can book one patient a week out of hours. Most of the theatre and ward staff know the routine. Mr Kirklan was just unlucky that there was no one available on the one day they were required.'

'You're being unreasonable, Abbey.'

'No, you're the one who's unreasonable. You pretend you want to help me turn this business around, but you storm in here complaining about everything I do or say. Quite honestly I'd be better off without your so-called help.'

He stared at her as if unable to believe his ears and she took advantage of his silence.

'Now, if you'd leave me to get on with *my* work, I'd appreciate it.'

'If that's the way you feel, I won't waste any more of *my* time either.' His voice was gruff as he tried to control his anger. 'But perhaps you'll allow me to mention one other thing before I leave. The hospital switchboard cannot cope. It needs replacing if you're not to lose business when calls can't get through immediately.'

Abbey sighed. 'I'm well aware of the shortcomings in that direction, and I can assure you that work is already in hand to improve things. Now, is there anything else, or can I get back to managing this hospital as I'm paid to do?'

'You can try, but unless you're prepared to address at least some of the issues we consultants raise you won't succeed. We all need to pull in the same direction to win, you know.' He strode from the room without a backward glance.

Sighing angrily, Abbey rose to close the door behind him. She poured herself a cup of coffee and tried to work out a strategy for coping with Max. As he was chairman of the MedCom she couldn't ignore him completely, but one thing she must do was ask Jane to keep him at bay as much as possible. And not just because he was repeatedly interrupting her work, but for her own peace of mind. For, as his temper had flared, his tensing muscles had emphasised his magnificent frame, making her heart race as she recalled what had once been between them.

When Jane brought in the mail on Friday morning, Abbey told her of her decision. 'From now on I'd appreciate it if you didn't allow Mr Darby anywhere near my office without my prior agreement.'

Jane looked troubled. 'He won't like that.'

'I know, but I think I need to make a stand. He seems to think I shouldn't do anything without consulting him first and that is not what I was appointed to do.'

'OK. I'll try. So long as you promise to have my injuries taken care of!' She laughed, but Abbey recognised the serious undertone in her words.

'Lay the blame at my door, but don't back down.'

Later, Abbey was eating her lunch in the staff dining room when he slid into the seat opposite. 'How goes it?'

'Fine,' she answered shortly.

'Why did you tell Jane to refuse me an appointment?'

'Because you've nothing constructive to say.'

'I didn't realise you were psychic,' he muttered, before adding, 'You can't keep on avoiding me. If nothing else, we need to discuss where we'll stay when we visit the Mercy next Friday.'

His supposition took her completely by surprise. 'What do you mean? It's not that far. I'm coming home the moment we're finished there.'

'But our appointment isn't until two-thirty and, rather than hare back fifty-odd miles on an empty stomach, I thought we could make arrangements to stay over locally.' He leaned confidingly across the table so that no-one else could hear. 'That way we can discuss the outcome of our visit before eating and while the afternoon's events are fresh in our minds.'

She remembered only too well the teasing, sensual smile that accompanied his words, and her heart longed to agree but was overruled by the necessity of keeping their relationship on a business footing. 'I would have thought we'd have done all the discussing needed during the afternoon.'

'But only in the presence of others. My guess is we'll have a lot to say to one another without anyone earwigging.'

'Max, I'm going to learn their business methods. I'm not sure why they've suggested you come along, but I hope it's so that you can meet their MedCom chairman and discover how you are expected to support the business rather than undermine it.'

He gave her a long, hard look. 'Are you suggesting I'm going about things the wrong way, then?' When she didn't answer, he leaned forward and said quietly, 'I spoke to Gordon Glennie and I don't think this is a learning experience for you. He said these visits are nearly always a waste of time. We'll be lectured by financial whizkids who will impress on us both that we must cut costs, but no one will give us a clue how to go about it.'

'Us?' Abbey queried coldly. 'I didn't think this was a joint appointment. I understood your job was to represent the medical staff using the hospital, not to balance my books. Much as I appreciate your support, I will not tolerate your interference. OK?'

'I get the message,' he told her huffily. 'You'd clearly rather struggle on alone, and as I have plenty to do I can assure you I won't force myself on you. Good afternoon.'

Despite the hurt she thought she read in his eyes, she didn't think for one moment that her frostiness would deter him for long, so she was more than a little surprised when he didn't appear for several days, and, quite unreasonably, she felt disappointed. However, it had its good side. With fewer interruptions, she achieved more by Wednesday than she'd managed since the day she started.

A quick ward round showed her that all was well with the patients, and she was especially pleased to see Mr Tate mobile and looking extremely well.

'You'll be going home soon, I guess.'

He nodded eagerly and joked, 'I can't wait to get out for that steak!'

'We'd better make sure the dietician sees you before you go. We don't want you back in because you've eaten the wrong things too soon.'

'Don't worry. I've more sense than that.' He gave her a cheery grin.

As she was about to leave the hospital that evening—promptly for once as she was meeting up with Cheryl—a patient was carried in through the main doors on a stretcher.

Waiting for the stretcher party to pass, Abbey was surprised to see Max's sister, Melissa, hovering anxiously over the patient. Worried in case it was Melissa's husband, Peter on the stretcher, Abbey approached quietly. 'Hello, Melissa.'

Flustered and obviously extremely anxious, Melissa spun round. 'Oh! It's you, Abbey. It—it's—this is Andy. My eldest. I—I can't believe this has happened.'

'What's the problem?' asked Abbey quietly, hoping to calm Melissa a little.

'The school. It's the school—they—' Melissa was near to tears.

'Let's get you through to an empty room.' Abbey spoke quickly to the girl on Reception and then asked the ambulance crew to take Andy through to an empty outpatient room.

The moment they were alone Melissa tried to finish her tale. 'The school took them to the dry ski slope this afternoon. Apparently a couple of the boys were messing about and Andy tried to avoid them and fell. The school rang me when they were back in Bleasdon and said his knee was swollen and who would I like him to see? Of course I said I would get him to Max, but by the time I arrived to collect Andy he could hardly walk so they called the ambulance.'

'Max knows you're here?'

Melissa shrugged. 'I hope so. His secretary said to bring Andy here and she'd contact Max in the meantime.'

Andy said, 'Stop fussing, Mum. He'll be here as soon as he can.'

Reluctant to get involved with an orthopaedic problem she knew little about, Abbey was nevertheless concerned that the boy seemed to be in a fair amount of pain. 'I'll get our own medical officer to come and see Andy,' she told them both, 'and then I'll try and contact Max—make sure he's got the message.'

Melissa nodded gratefully. 'Thanks. I—I don't know where he—'

'Don't worry,' Abbey told her. 'We have ways and means of finding him.'

Abbey made her way back to her office and asked the receptionist to bleep Max while she herself phoned Ellie. 'Max Darby's sister is in Outpatients with her son. He's damaged his knee and seems rather uncomfortable. Would you mind having a look at him and see if he needs anything done until I can locate Max?'

'Sure—Max's nephew, you say? I'll be glad to. What's his name?'

'Andy Barnes.' Having replaced the receiver, she drummed her fingers on the desk as she waited for

Max to return her call. When, after several minutes, she'd heard nothing, she rang the receptionist again. 'Haven't you managed to contact Mr Darby yet?'

'I've bleeped him three times and there's been no response. I've tried to ring his secretary, too, but her phone's been constantly engaged.'

'Give me his secretary's number and I'll keep trying.' She guessed the girl had enough to do without that as well.

When she had scribbled down the number she was given, Abbey had another thought. 'Mr Darby has a mobile phone. Do you have that number?'

The receptionist was hesitant. 'I do, yes, but we've been banned from using them since they discovered the effect on the cardiac monitors and such like.'

'Give it to me. I'll try it.'

The girl did so willingly, relieved that she wasn't being asked to break the rules.

Abbey tried Max's secretary first but with the same result as the receptionist. She then dialled the number of his mobile phone and counted the rings impatiently. Eleven. Twelve. Where on earth could he be?

'Hello,' a soft voice greeted her. 'Who's speaking?'

Abbey recognised immediately that it was Helen and had to swallow hard before she could say evenly, 'Abbey Westray speaking. From St Luke's. Is Max there, Helen? I need to get a message to him urgently.'

Helen was obviously unhappy at being recognised as she stuttered, 'Oh—er—yes. Well—err—he is here, but he can't come to the phone at the moment. But I can give him a message?' she offered.

Puzzled by Helen's behaviour, Abbey could only think that the sister was embarrassed that she, the hospital manager, had discovered them together. 'Tell him that his sister, Melissa, is at St Luke's with her son, Andy. He's injured his knee. His secretary was supposed to be contacting him so he might know already, but I think Andy is in quite a lot of pain.'

'Er—I don't think he knows. His phone and bleeper have been—well—unattended for the past hour or so. I'll—er—I'll tell him.' Her wariness changed to relief as she added, 'In fact he's here now.'

Abbey heard Helen give Max a quick résumé of what she'd said, then he took the receiver, sounding as cagey as Helen. 'Er—I—er—I'll come right over, Abbey. Er—is he in any pain?'

Surprised by his unusual indecision, she tried to reassure him about his nephew's condition. 'I think perhaps he is, although he's putting a brave face on it. However, I've asked Ellie to check him.'

'That's great, thanks. She'll know what to do.'

'Your secretary's been trying to reach you about this as well. Would you like me to contact her?'

'I'd be very grateful, Abbey, then I can come right over immediately.' He ended the call and Abbey was left looking at the dead receiver.

Having eventually succeeded in contacting Max's secretary, and discovering that her phone had been continuously engaged because she had spent nearly an hour trying to contact Max, Abbey felt despondent. Whatever else she thought about him, she'd always considered Max conscientious. Because he cared about his patients, he used to make sure he could be reached at any time. Now it seemed that Helen was more important.

Trying to tell herself that it was none of her business, she returned to the outpatient department and told Ellie and Melissa that Max was on his way.

'Where from?' Ellie wanted to know.

'I didn't ask.' She didn't want to admit that he hadn't given her the opportunity.

'That's a pity, because if he's not coming from far away I'd rather wait for his opinion.'

'He didn't sound as if it would take long to get here.'

In which case, guessing that he'd bring Helen with him, Abbey didn't want to be there when they arrived. That would be pushing her emotions too far!

She smiled at Melissa. 'Before I go, can I offer you some tea or coffee? Obviously we can't let Andy have anything until we see if he needs to go to Theatre.'

'No, thanks. I'll wait and see what Max says.'

'Right. I hope everything goes OK. Sorry I have to dash, but I've arranged to meet someone this evening.' She hurried out to the car park, fervently hoping she wouldn't meet them on the way.

She was lucky, and arrived home to find Cheryl waiting on the doorstep. 'Come on in. Sorry to be late. I won't be a moment changing.'

Having booked a table at a swish new restaurant that had just opened nearby, Abbey was determined not to ruin the outing for Cheryl and so put on a happy front for the evening. Over a meal of pasta dishes, they laughed ceaselessly as Abbey reminded Cheryl of some of the antics they had got up to in their schooldays.

However, once they were on their respective ways home Abbey's mood changed completely. The confirmation of Max's relationship with Helen dashed any hope she still had that she was wrong about their relationship. She felt as if a light had been switched off in her life.

As she locked up for the night, the telephone rang. She answered it cautiously.

'Hi, Abbey.' She was surprised to hear Max's voice. 'I just wanted to thank you for what you did this evening.'

'It was nothing,' she demurred.

'Your just being there helped Melissa. She was confident that you would get things organised. Goodness knows how long it might have been until I knew about Andy if you hadn't rung.'

She wanted to ask what he expected if he left his bleeper and telephone unattended, but instead she asked, 'How is he?'

'Not very comfortable—I've put him in a plaster of Paris cylinder.'

'What do you think the problem is?'

'Looks like torn ligaments. The anterior cruciates, to be exact. I should think he'll need to keep the plaster cast on for three weeks or so. I'm keeping him in overnight in case the swelling causes a problem. It's lucky half-term's coming up so he won't miss too much school.'

'What about his skiing holiday?'

'That could be a problem. We'll just have to wait and see how quickly it heals.'

'Poor lad. He'll be disappointed.' Abbey laughed, then added, 'I did warn you about the dry ski slopes!'

Abbey had made the statement as a joke between friends, but Max retorted defensively, 'Accidents like this are no laughing matter. They can happen anywhere when people mess about. I suspect the teachers weren't keeping a close enough eye on them.'

'I wasn't criticising, Max,' she assured him. 'It was just a throw-away comment.'

He was silent for a moment. 'I guess I overreacted because I'm tired and worried. Anyway, before I took Melissa home I tried to ring you but you weren't in. This is the first chance I've had since to ring and thank you.'

'There was no need.'

'I think there was,' he answered affably. 'Have you eaten?'

'Yes. At the new Italian place near here.'

'In that case perhaps I could treat you to a meal another night?'

Abbey couldn't believe her ears. Did he think she would be grateful for the crumbs from Helen's table?

Or was he worried that, after Helen had answered his mobile phone, Abbey would not succumb to his cajolery in the future?

'There's no need for that, Max. Thanks for the thought, though, and have a good night.'

He gave an audible sigh and she wondered why. She couldn't believe that her reluctance to become involved on a personal level was the cause. However, if Max thought so, he gave no indication of it when he said, 'In that case I'll say goodnight. And thanks once again.'

Abbey spent a troubled night as she tried to understand exactly why she felt so unsettled by his call. She'd done nothing that evening to warrant such effusive thanks or the offer of a meal. And he already had Helen. So what did he want with her as well?

CHAPTER FIVE

ABBEY went straight to the wards when she arrived at work on Thursday morning. 'How is Andy Barnes this morning?' she asked Penny.

'He's gone home.'

'Gone home?' Abbey stared at the nurse, her eyes wide with disbelief.

'Yes. Mr Darby came in early with his sister and he arranged for Andy to be transported home.'

'Was there a problem?'

'No. Not that I'm aware of. The lad slept well and seemed much more comfortable.'

As it was still only nine o'clock, Abbey wondered what the hurry had been. However, there was nothing more she could do there so she went up to her office.

Throughout the morning she half expected Max or even Melissa to let her know how Andy was progressing, but she heard nothing. She guessed it was probably her own fault for being so indifferent when Max had telephoned the night before.

When she saw Ellie at lunchtime, she asked her if Andy had had a good night.

'Yes, fine. He was no trouble at all. I don't think the injury is that serious, really. Perhaps Max was embarrassed by his sister's fussing?'

'Even so, it was a bit over the top for Max to whisk him away so early.'

Ellie shrugged. 'He's a busy man. I suppose he wanted to see him settled before he started his day proper. I'd been up in the night so was still asleep when he came in, but I do know his sister was reluctant to leave the lad here the night before so I guess she kept on at him.'

'Why didn't she want to leave him? They seemed very pleased with her husband's treatment here.'

Ellie laughed. 'Probably her guilt at sending him away to boarding-school! I shouldn't worry about it.'

'I won't.' But nevertheless Abbey couldn't accept that that could be the reason. She even began to wonder if the real reason he had rung the previous evening was to explain where he and Helen had been earlier. She could only imagine that as she hadn't made it easy for him he hadn't known what to say to her.

So she was totally bemused when she came in early on Friday morning and found an arrangement of red roses on her desk. Wondering if this was another thank-you from the Barnes family, she searched around until she found a card.

It read, 'I'll pick you up around twelve. Hope you've brought your toothbrush. Max.' No mention of Andy.

She slid the card under her blotter as Jane came in with the post. 'Ooh, you've got a Valentine present. They're lovely.'

Not having given a thought to what day it was, Abbey had believed they were intended as an apology. She felt her colour rising. 'They're nice, but I don't think they can be for me.'

'Is there a card?'

Abbey made a pretence of searching through the foliage. 'No. Can't see one.'

'An unknown admirer. How exciting. It can't be a mistake because your name's plain enough on the door.'

'Yes, well. I'll enjoy them until lunchtime, then you can have the benefit of them for the afternoon.'

'Oh, can't you take them with you? Your admirer *will* be disappointed.'

Abbey laughed. 'He should have checked my diary,

then. Now, we must get down to work because Mr
Darby is collecting me at twelve.'

'Ooh,' Jane breathed. 'You don't think they're from
him, do you?'

'Certainly not. He's the one person who knows I
won't be in the office this afternoon.' The last thing
she wanted was to be the subject of hospital gossip—
rumours spread like wild fire in places like St Luke's.
'Anyway, whoever sent them, I must get on—I've a
lot to do in a short morning.'

'I nearly forgot—Mr Brewton has made an appointment to see you at eleven.'

'Good. Perhaps we can secure his services for
St Luke's once and for all. Did he say anything more?'

'It was his secretary who rang. She was surprised
that you'd asked to see him. She said managers usually
tried to keep as far away from medics as possible.'

'I don't know where they've got these ideas from.
If it wasn't for them the rest of us would be out of a
job, wouldn't we?'

'Oh, yes, but then I think because you were a nurse
you approach the job differently.'

'Maybe that's it. I wonder if the consultants approve
or disapprove?'

'Approve, I should think. At least they're able to
put forward their point of view.'

Abbey shrugged. 'I wonder! Time will no doubt tell.
Now, anything else? No word from Mr Inklin, I
suppose?'

Jane shook her head. 'Afraid not.' She opened the
door. 'Buzz me if you want anything.'

The moment Jane had closed the door behind her,
Abbey retrieved the card that had come with the
flowers and pushed it into the deepest part of her
handbag.

Eleven o'clock arrived far too quickly. Her gaze
repeatedly strayed to the flowers, causing distracting

thoughts of Max and preventing her from concentrating.

However, she knew it was essential to give her visitor her undivided attention, and, moving the arrangement, she resolutely turned her back on the flowers.

'Pleased to meet you, Mr Brewton,' she greeted him when Jane brought him through. 'Coffee?' She was delighted to discover that he was one of the senior surgeons and appeared genuinely pleased to meet her.

'Great.' His friendly face beamed his thanks.

She handed him a cup. 'I gather you had a problem trying to book theatre time the other morning?'

'It's something that's happened once or twice recently, but when Max told me you were happy for us to take patients to the Cotswold until the staffing levels could be sorted out I did just that.'

'He said what?' Abbey couldn't believe her ears.

He grinned again. 'Of course he knows the moment you're back into full swing again I'll be back. I'd much rather work here.'

Relieved, Abbey swallowed the protest she had been about to make. 'I'm pleased to hear it.' She went on to explain to Mr Brewton that she was doing to remedy the situation and how soon she hoped things would improve.

To her relief, he was extremely amenable and before he left reiterated again that he had no intention of deserting St Luke's permanently.

When Max arrived to pick her up she glared at him accusingly. 'What do you mean by telling consultants to take their work to the Cotswold?'

He grinned sheepishly. 'I didn't do that, Abbey. All I said—'

'All you said was, "Go there this time and then I can put pressure on the manager to find us more staff immediately." Well, I've seen through your scheming. It won't work. Not for your reasons, anyway.'

He grinned engagingly. 'It's made you think and that's all I intended.'

Abbey shook her head as she shuffled her papers together and locked them away.

'How's Andy?'

'He's OK. Melissa is fussing over him like a mother hen.'

'You certainly sneaked him out early yesterday!'

'I didn't sneak him out,' he protested. 'Melissa came in with me and, finding him much more comfortable, we decided to make the move. All the arrangements just fell into place very easily.'

'I thought perhaps we hadn't been looking after him to your satisfaction,' she told him wryly.

He appeared genuinely surprised at her even considering such an idea. 'That's ridiculous. I just wanted to see him settled so I could forget about him while I got on with everything else I had to do.'

'You might have let me know that was the reason!'

'I didn't think you were particularly interested.'

So her apparent indifference *had* upset him? 'I'm interested in all the patients here.'

'Of course. You're still a nurse at heart, aren't you? Now, where's your overnight bag?'

Annoyed at his taking the opportunity to have another dig at her, she retorted, 'I told you, I'm coming back to the flat.'

Ignoring her protest, he told her, 'We'll collect it on the way. That's why I left plenty of time.'

She picked up the flowers. 'I'll just take these in to Jane.'

'Why?' He took them from her and placed them on the desk. 'They're for you. Not Jane. We can drop them off when we pick up your case.'

Abbey felt her colour rising. 'Thank you for the thought, Max, but it wasn't necessary.'

He stopped her in her tracks and grasped her upper

arms. 'Why not, Abbey? Despite your position you're a very attractive woman and deserve to be spoiled. Why shouldn't you receive flowers from an eligible male for once? Especially on Valentine's Day.'

Wanting to vehemently deny that receiving flowers was an unusual occurrence, she tried to avoid his searching gaze but he trapped her face between his hands. 'Why the barriers, Abbey?'

Overwhelming misery prevented her from answering. If he couldn't see what an insult it was, sending her flowers because he thought no one else would, how could she ever explain her need to keep him at arm's length?

For a brief time that morning she'd nearly convinced herself that the flowers indicated that she meant more to him than she believed but once again he had dashed any hope of that.

He actually felt sorry for her and expected her to grab at whatever he offered. He was wrong. She wanted something more than a casual relationship, especially one that would undermine the position she had worked so hard to achieve.

When she didn't speak, he sighed deeply and released his hold. She seized the opportunity to buzz Jane on the intercom. 'I'm leaving now, Jane. Could you let Security know that I'll collect my car later? I'm not sure what time. Depends when the meeting ends. Have a good weekend. I'll see you on Monday.'

Lifting the file of papers she had prepared earlier for her discussion at the Mercy, she set off down the corridor. Max picked up the flowers and followed.

Noticing, she ordered sharply, 'Leave the flowers with Jane.' She could just imagine the rumours that would circulate if they were seen leaving the hospital together, Max carrying red roses, on Valentine's Day!

As they crossed the car park, he took the file from her arms, and when they reached his car, locked it in the boot. When she was seated beside him he asked tersely, 'Why didn't you tell Jane I sent the flowers?'

'You know as well as I do what hospital staff are like for putting two and two together and making five.'

'Would it matter?'

'Of course it would,' she snapped. 'It wouldn't do either of us any good and you should know that perfectly well.' Suddenly recognising that they were not on the road to the Mercy, she asked, 'Where are we going?'

'We need to eat and the Spread Eagle does good bar food.'

She frowned. 'Where's that?'

'Just around the corner from your flat. Do you mean to say you haven't tried it?'

'I don't frequent pubs much.'

'No? Hospital managers can no doubt afford swish new Italian restaurants. Is that where you eat with lover boy, then?'

After his earlier unchivalrous comments, Abbey decided that it would be a good idea to prolong her deception. 'We ate at his place. And I'd rather you didn't call him "lover boy".'

'What else would I call him—you've no rings, so I presume he's not your husband, or fiancé?'

'His name's Ben. The way you go on about him, anyone would think you are jealous.'

'Not any more, but I was when I discovered you'd been two-timing me all those years ago.'

Abbey was outraged. 'I didn't two-time you.'

'You didn't? That's hard for me to accept when I believe you're not the kind of person to move in with someone you'd only just met.' He looked at her keenly.

Fuming, Abbey retorted, 'Of course I hadn't just met him. We went to school together.'

'I see.' His tone was icy. 'That's two-timing in my book.'

Abbey was so angry at his accusation that she made up her mind that there was no way she was going to enlighten him. Ever. Let him go on thinking what he liked.

'You promised to let me know where you were working. When I didn't hear from you, did you expect me to sit and wait until chance threw us together again?'

He had pulled the car to a stop outside her flat as she spoke. He leaned across and, opening the passenger door, said quietly, 'Grab your overnight bag. And hurry. Otherwise we'll have to eat standing up. The Eagle's popular.'

Angry that he'd ignored her outburst, Abbey closed the door again. 'I don't need my bag. I'm coming home.'

'It's just a precaution in case we're delayed. Now we're here, you may as well collect it.'

Unwilling to have an argument with him on her doorstep, Abbey did as he said, but she was determined that she would not be dictated to.

A toothbrush, he'd said. A toothbrush she would take! She tossed it into her otherwise empty bag, which she then snapped closed before slamming the door and rejoining him in the car.

As Max had predicted, the Spread Eagle was full and they had to share a table with two estate agents, so conversation was general. But she did agree with him on one thing. The food was worth it.

She enjoyed a seafood cannelloni, exquisitely seasoned with just the right amount of basil, and Max chose a smoked salmon pasta dish topped with a creamy wine sauce.

When they had both finished every morsel, he looked at his watch. 'One o'clock. We need to make a move if we're not going to be late.'

They made their farewells and Max led the way across the car park.

'Oh, no. Look at that.'

'What? Oh, Max. Your car—what's happened? It looks—'

'Someone's reversed into the door.'

'Oh, Max.'

'And left no note. People are the pits sometimes.' He unlocked the driver's door and opened it. 'Oh, well, at least it still opens, and it'll mend, I suppose, but it's damned annoying.'

He drove in silence until they were out of the town and then, turning to look at her, said, 'Truce?'

She kept her eyes down as she said, 'OK—for the sake of the business.'

'For the sake of the business,' he assured her gravely. 'It would look bad if we arrived at the Mercy not speaking to one another, wouldn't it?'

Abbey looked up at him and nearly threw away any advantage she might have gained by almost laughing. His eyes were concentrating on the road ahead, but a satisfied grin lightened his features to such an extent that she saw once again the young senior house officer she had loved so dearly.

Reluctantly tearing her eyes away, she broke the silence by saying, 'We'll be there in good time, won't we?'

Max nodded, and flashed an amused glance towards her. 'You're tense again. Because you're still angry with me, or is it the thought of the meetings ahead?'

She made a conscious attempt to relax. 'Neither. You're imagining things.'

'Hmm.'

She turned to look at him again. 'What does that mean?'

'It means I don't believe you, but it's not important. OK?'

Perversely disappointed by his professed lack of interest, she agreed. 'OK.' There was nothing more she could add. She was too confused by the rapid changes in his manner towards her—one moment appearing to consider her a friend, if not something more, the next making it clear that she was nothing more than a business colleague.

The ensuing silence was broken by Max as he drove through the main gateway of the Mercy hospital. 'Where do we have to report?'

'Er—Group Admin, I suppose.' Abbey gestured towards a sign. 'That must be it, over to the right.'

Max drove past the modern hospital building towards the beautifully proportioned Victorian stone building she'd indicated. 'They certainly do themselves proud,' he muttered as he parked the car.

Abbey glanced around. Even from the outside it was obvious that no expense had been spared on the building, and that rankled when she thought of the parsimonious budget she was allowed for maintenance at St Luke's. However, she defended her employers loyally. 'In business it's important to make a good impression.'

'Not on me it isn't,' he whispered as they walked into a lushly carpeted hall lit by a magnificent crystal chandelier.

'Can I help you?' The smartly dressed receptionist sprang to her feet from behind a word processor.

'We have a two-thirty appointment. With Mr Barratt, I believe,' Abbey told her. 'We're from St Luke's.'

The girl nodded knowledgeably. 'He's expecting you.' She led them down a luxuriously fitted-out corridor and knocked on the end door.

'Come in Miss Westray.' Abbey saw that it was the chairman of her interview panel. 'And Mr Darby, isn't it?' Mr Barratt strode forward with his hand out-stretched.

'Pleased to meet you.' Max shook the proffered

hand, then ushered Abbey over to a comfortable seat.

'I'll just buzz Mr Ambrose. He chairs the Mercy MedCom, so we thought it would be a good opportunity for you to meet him. He's come in specially.' He beamed at them both. 'Now, while we're waiting, let me give you a general idea of our aims for St Luke's.'

Max raised an amused eyebrow towards Abbey as Mr Barratt outlined the way he thought the business should be growing and what the consultants could do to help, especially in the way of cutting costs.

Finding it hard not to join in his amusement, Abbey was relieved when Max was whisked away by his medical colleague—leaving her to a gruelling interrogation as to the present state of business at St Luke's. Mr Barratt then moved on to enquire how she intended to change things.

Eventually her tormentor warned her, 'You must cut, cut, cut costs. We cannot continue to subsidise St Luke's the way we are.'

Abbey was again tempted to grin as she recalled Max saying that that was what she would be told to do. 'I'm not sure that I can cut them much further.'

'But you must. We expect it of you.'

'How?'

'That's for you to decide, my dear. That's why we appointed you as manager. If you think it's more than you can cope with, perhaps you should see how the Mercy goes about it.'

'Perhaps I should.' She knew it was pointless arguing or even complaining that she hadn't been given the full picture at her interview. Mr Barratt was making it clear that it was now up to her to do something about it or give way to someone who would.

Abbey suddenly wished that she hadn't rejected Max's help so forcibly. When she'd started at St Luke's, she hadn't realised how lonely life as a hospital manager would be. She had no one to turn to for support when the situation became difficult, no one to chew things over with.

How stupid she had been.

Mr Barratt escorted her over to the main hospital building and introduced her to Bob Holland, the manager.

The moment the door closed behind her tormentor, Bob Holland grinned. 'You need to cut costs and you've been told I am the man to show you how. Right?'

Abbey nodded hesitantly, unsure how to react to his apparently irreverent statement.

'Don't take it to heart, Miss Westray.'

'Do call me Abbey.'

'And I'm Bob. Well, Abbey, no matter how successful you are, they'll keep the pressure on for you to do more while they spend the hard-won proceeds.' He laughed. 'In a couple of months you'll ignore them, like I do. I'll willingly show you my accounts, but it won't help you a bit. I'm quite sure costs are pared to the bone at St Luke's already.'

Abbey grinned then as she recognised Bob as a comrade in adversity! He had been, and probably still was, under as much pressure as she felt at that moment. 'I'm glad to hear you say that. It's all a bit unfair, isn't it?'

'Health is a cutthroat business these days. However, it might help if I show you how I do creative accounting to keep them quiet. It's a bit of a fiddle, but stops some of the interfering.'

Abbey learnt a lot from Bob that afternoon, and by the time Max and John Ambrose, a general surgeon, came in search of her she was feeling quite relaxed.

'Let's go over to the canteen for a cuppa,' John suggested. 'Max and I have talked ourselves dry.'

Abbey nodded. 'I know the feeling.'

The conversation between them flowed so freely

that it was way after six by the time Abbey and Max left the Mercy.

He grimaced as they made their way to the car park. 'Apart from the socialising, that was a total waste of time.'

Abbey disagreed. 'Not as far as I'm concerned. I've learnt a lot.'

'Such as?'

'How to keep the financial wizards off my back and, even more important, that there's someone at the Mercy I can turn to when the going gets too tough.'

Max shook his head. 'Ah. So you accept now that it will get tough? I told you this job wasn't right for you. You're an innocent amongst business sharks. You should be doing what you're best at: nursing. Not trying to run the world.'

'I needed a challenge.'

'Well, I should say you've certainly got one. I wouldn't trust that Mr Barratt further than I could throw him. I would have liked to have stayed and heard what he expects of you, but it's just as well I didn't. I'd probably have let you down by telling him a few home truths.'

She laughed. 'You already know what he said, anyway—that I should cut, cut, cut costs and then continue cutting.'

'How dare he sit in that luxuriously appointed office and tell you to make more savings? The contrasts in that place made my blood boil. I think we need something to take away the taste of corrupt commercialism as soon as we can. Perhaps we should make a night of it after all?'

Abbey ignored his tentative suggestion. 'Corrupt? That's a bit over the top, Max. It is a business, after all, and if they don't make a profit they'll soon go bust.'

'I know that. But I'm not sure I like the way they go about it. That's all I'm saying, so you can stop defending them so loyally. I don't believe they'd do the same for you if the occasion arose. If you don't do exactly as they say, my guess is you'll be out on your ear.'

'Thanks for the vote of confidence.'

'Don't get me wrong, Abbey. I'm not questioning your ability, just their methods. But don't let's argue over them. They aren't worth it. I think we should forget all about the visit and decide where to go next.'

Abbey surreptitiously checked her watch before saying firmly, 'I told you, Max, I'd prefer to go home. Especially now you've decided we won't talk about the visit.'

'OK.' Max raised his hands defensively. 'I'll take you home, but later. First I'm going to treat you to that slap-up meal I promised—to prevent you going back to an empty flat and worrying over what you've been ordered to do.'

'I really ought to get back, Max.' The temptation to agree, to mull over what had happened with someone who understood, was strong but she was still hesitant to trust herself in his company for too long.

He must have recognised that she was wavering and pressed his advantage. 'Surely we can share a meal first? Please, Abbey. I'd like a chance to talk to you without interruption, and right away from the unreal situation we find ourselves in at St Luke's.'

'What do you mean, "unreal"?' she retorted sharply, wondering why she had, even briefly, considered confiding in him. 'You just can't accept my position, can you?'

'Abbey,' he responded quietly, 'if it's what you want I don't mind at all. But I don't think it *is* making you happy. And, contrary to what you seem to think, your happiness is important to me.'

Startled, Abbey raised her eyes to meet his, hoping to discover if he really meant what he was saying. What she did find was an unexpected tenderness in their depths.

'So will you stay and eat with me?' His quiet sincerity was having a devastating effect on her resolution, but, remembering that he had been with Helen when she had rung on Wednesday, she found it difficult to rid herself of the suspicion that he was still trying to get round her for purely selfish reasons.

However, her resolve suddenly crumbled and she capitulated with a smile. 'I'd like that, Max. Thank you.' And I hope I don't regret it, she told herself silently.

CHAPTER SIX

Max helped Abbey into his car and, starting the engine, took the road that ran in the totally opposite direction to Bleasdon.

'Where are we going?'

'To a very special country hotel I know of. It's called the Arbour.' A few minutes later he swung into an almost empty car park attached to an enormous granite house which was surrounded by pergolas.

'It's lovely, Max. I bet it's a picture when all the climbers are in bloom.'

'It certainly is. And because so many of the plants are old-fashioned varieties the mingled scents are out of this world. Perhaps we could come again in the summer and see them? When the roses are out is the best time.'

When she didn't answer, he murmured, 'I knew you'd like it. It's your kind of place. It's where I'd planned to stay tonight. If you'd agreed, that is.'

Abbey felt as if all her breath had been knocked from her body at the thought of him wanting them to stay together at somewhere so special to him. *And* suggesting that she return there with him later in the year.

Again she wondered if she'd misjudged him from the start. Was her fear of becoming involved a second time making her blind to the truth? She couldn't believe so when the evidence of his relationship with Helen was only too obvious. And yet nothing about his behaviour seemed to add up.

She would have been only too happy if she could have believed that he wanted something more than a repeat of their previous transient affair. But she couldn't. And if that was all he was offering it was not enough. She could not endure a resurgence of the bleak pain that had torn her apart the last time.

Attempting to give him the benefit of the doubt, she raised her eyes to meet his and half smiled as she asked suspiciously, 'Why is this place so special?'

'You'll see.' Her eyes were momentarily held by his and she felt a sudden surge of fire touch each of her nerve-endings in turn.

She caught her breath and, to escape the intensity of the moment, opened the passenger door. As they walked towards the hotel entrance he told her, 'The food and the service here are what make it so special.'

He crossed to Reception and booked a table for seven-fifteen, then led the way to a sumptuous lounge bar.

'What would you like to drink?'

Determined to keep a clear head, she asked for tonic water with lemon and ice, then, noting the smartly dressed customers around them, asked, 'Do you mind if I freshen up before we eat?'

'Not at all. Shall I get your bag from the car?'

Recognising that it wasn't a good time for him to discover that there was nothing more than a toothbrush in it, Abbey shook her head. 'I'll get it.'

He handed her the keys and, after going to the car, she made her way to the cloakroom with her overnight bag containing just her toothbrush.

Max was waiting with the drinks when she returned, and appeared to have tidied himself up in the meantime.

'I haven't taken my bag back as I thought you might be about to do the same, but I see I'm too late. I'll just return it to the car.'

'No need.' Max had risen to his feet at her approach. 'It'll be all right in Reception until we're ready to leave.' As he took the bag from her hand, he raised a surprised eyebrow. 'My word, you travel light.'

She watched as he exchanged pleasantries with the receptionist, grateful that those few moments were enough for the guilty colour to subside from her cheeks.

Over drinks, Max told her what he had learnt about the Mercy from John Ambrose. 'They had the same problem as St Luke's in the beginning: too few staff to encourage the consultants to move there. But unlike us they had little competition, so the business grew quite quickly.'

Abbey filled in a lot of the gaps with what she had learnt from Bob Holland. 'He doesn't let them see the proper accounts. Just a sanitised version. It seems to work, allowing enough latitude for the hospital business to grow.'

All the time that she was speaking she was conscious of Max's close scrutiny of her. A scrutiny that made her uncomfortably aware that she really knew nothing more about this man than she had all those years before.

And, when she thought about it, that was precious little. She'd considered his physical attraction more than enough so she'd never tried to discover what lay below the surface.

When the waiter brought the menu, she was overwhelmed by the choice. 'Where do we start?'

'I think I remember your tastes pretty well,' he told her quietly, 'and I can safely say there's very little on that menu you won't enjoy, apart from the calamari.'

He laughed. 'And that's because I recall an evening in a very smart Greek restaurant when you announced at the top of your voice that you didn't expect to be fed rubber tyres at that price!'

Abbey felt the colour scald her cheeks as she remembered the fuss she'd made. 'I'm better behaved these days. I promise there won't be a repetition.'

'I should hope not,' he teased.

When they'd ordered, Max sat back and, watching her closely, said quietly, 'I've been waiting for this opportunity since I learned you were going to be the new manager.'

'What do you mean, "opportunity"?' Abbey asked guardedly.

'St Luke's was the last place I expected to find you. I imagined you a harassed mum with several blue-eyed, blond troublemakers.' He smiled lazily, but whether it was at his mental picture or because he now knew his vision had been wrong she couldn't decide. 'When I heard about your appointment, I looked forward to meeting up with you again. When soon afterwards I was elected to the chair of the MedCom, it seemed Lady Luck was taking a hand.'

'Luck?' Sensing a hidden agenda in his voice, she countered, 'I would have called it fate.' She nearly qualified the noun with 'malicious', but thought better of it.

He held her gaze with his dark eyes and replied, 'Whichever, it doesn't really matter what you call it. It just seemed we were being given the perfect opportunity to renew our friendship, starting where we left off.'

Abbey tried to read the truth in his eyes, but his unwavering stare told her nothing. Her suspicions were aroused again.

Hadn't he threatened in the beginning to fight her all the way? Having discovered that she didn't respond to intimidation, was he still trying to get round her in other ways? Maybe it wasn't ten years too late as far as she was concerned, but for Max it was. She was quite sure that Helen was not his only conquest in that time. Having seen him in action with Ellie, it was obvious that he was a seasoned campaigner.

'I'm quite happy to be friends,' she offered cautiously.

'But nothing more?'

She shrugged noncommittally.

'Because of the guy you were at school with?'

Abbey knew that this was probably the best opportunity she would have to set the record straight, but, unable to accept Max's words at face value, she feared that once she admitted the truth she would be at his mercy. The only way she could survive working so closely with him was to keep Ben as a useful shield for her true feelings.

'I suppose that's one reason.'

His gaze moved pointedly to the empty fingers of her left hand, and he said quietly, 'But it's not good enough for me.'

'Maybe not, but there are others. Ten years is a long time, Max. Things can never be the same. We've both had experiences that must have made us different people. I don't think I really know you any more.'

'Maybe, but there's a lot that hasn't changed, and I give you fair warning—' he lowered his voice seductively '—I intend to get to know the parts of *you* that have.'

The quivering excitement that rippled through her veins in response to his declaration was so unsettling that she decided to treat what he'd said as a joke. 'I shouldn't hold your breath, Max.'

He didn't laugh, rather raised his eyes to search her face, revealing a hint of exasperation that increased Abbey's unease.

However, their starters arrived at that moment, so the subject was dropped in favour of enjoyment of the food.

'These are fantastic,' Abbey told him enthusiastically as she tasted the prawns marinated in a tantalising

Pernod-flavoured sauce. 'Incredible, really. And the bread. It's out of this world.'

'All baked on the premises. It is every bit as special as I said, isn't it?'

Abbey had to agree. 'This starter would usually be a whole meal for me! I hope I can manage the next course.'

'You'd better,' he said with a grin, 'or you'll hurt the chef's feelings. He's not used to having any of his food returned. Anyway, I don't believe you eat enough for someone working the long hours you do.'

'I don't have such a big frame as you to fill!'

He nodded his agreement and Abbey felt a companionable ambience envelop them.

The whole meal was everything Max had predicted, and more. He even persuaded her to try a glass of wine with the garlic- and herb-stuffed lamb she had ordered. 'For your digestion's sake, to paraphrase Timothy.'

She laughed then. 'I'd forgotten your regular quotes from the Bible.'

He leaned across and took her hands in his. 'I think there's a lot you've forgotten about me.'

She tried to pull away, but he resisted. 'I wish I'd been able to forget you as easily.'

Wanting to believe him, she very nearly admitted that it had been anything but easy, but was prevented from doing so by an insistent inner voice asking why she thought she could trust him this time.

To lessen the intensity of the moment, she asked, 'Is your father still a chaplain in the army?'

Obviously disappointed by her not responding as he'd hoped, he sighed and released her hands. 'No, he's retired and he and Mum live near Mel. He still takes the occasional service, but he doesn't have a regular commitment.'

'I'd like to hear him preach sometime. He was

overseas when I knew you before, so I never got the chance.'

Obviously unhappy at the way she'd diverted the conversation, he uttered a sigh of resignation before saying, 'If you really mean it, I'll invite you to his next service.'

She smiled warmly. 'Thanks. I wouldn't have said it if I hadn't meant it.'

'I wonder.' Their coffee was taken through to the lounge as he voiced his obvious doubt, so it was with his reply hanging between them that he led the way to a seat by the blazing log fire. 'Now, can we forget our respective parents for the moment and get back to discussing us?'

He must have noticed a shadow flit across Abbey's face at his remark. 'I'm sorry, Abbey.' He was clearly contrite. 'I haven't enquired after your family.'

Abbey studiously examined her nails. 'Dad died many years ago. Mum has moved in with an old school-friend who needed help on her smallholding. I see her when I can, but the journey isn't easy.'

He leaned towards her sympathetically. 'I'm sorry to hear that, Abbey. I'd no idea. You were very close to your father, weren't you?'

'I was, yes. Losing him made me even more determined to work for improvements in patient care.'

Max regarded her thoughtfully. 'Are you implying that poor nursing cost him his life?'

'No way. His brain tumour proved to be malignant and inoperable so his death was pretty inevitable.'

Taking one of her hands between his, Max gently traced circles on her palm with his thumb. Abbey guessed that he was only trying to convey his sympathy, but the movement was so erotic that something inside her ached for more and she had to stop him before she made a fool of herself.

She caught both his hands with hers. 'It was a long

time ago, Max, and I've come to terms with it. But, as you say, I still miss him.'

She pulled right away from him then and lifted her cup of coffee in a protective gesture.

When he didn't speak, but held her eyes with a penetrating stare that had an even more devastating effect on her than any words, she was sure that he must sense her body's strong attraction towards him and spoke in a desperate effort to break the spell he was casting on her.

'You mentioned the other day that time Mum and I visited him in hospital and felt that not enough was being done for the patients. He was lucky, and soon came home. Many of them didn't, and I know that both he and Mum wished there was something they could do to change things. I'm hoping to do it for them.'

He shook his head regretfully. 'Why do you shy away like a startled horse every time I bring the discussion round to you and me?'

'I don't.' She closed her eyes. This was even worse than she'd feared. Why ever had she agreed to come?

'I'm worried about you, Abbey,' he murmured gently. 'I don't believe I've seen you relax since you started at St Luke's. It's not doing you any good, you know. I want to see the sparkle of fun that always used to shine in your eyes.'

'I was young and carefree then, Max. Now I have responsibilities and I've told you what I'm trying to achieve.'

'We all tend to be idealists in the medical world,' Max told her quietly, 'but in the end we have to accept that health care costs money and there isn't enough of it to go round. As I suspect you're beginning to find out.'

'At least in this job I can make sure that what there is is spent wisely.'

He nodded and smiled indulgently. 'You can certainly try.'

'But you don't think I'll succeed?'

'I wouldn't go so far as to say that, but your campaigning could probably be put to better use.'

'Such as?' she queried sceptically.

Max regarded her thoughtfully for a moment, then, appearing to come to a decision, asked, 'Would you like to know what I've been doing over the past ten years or so?'

Uncomfortably aware that in those few moments of silence he'd made the decision to tell her something he hadn't intended to, Abbey murmured, 'To get where you are today, you must have been concentrating on your career. I guess you've been studying for a large part of the time.'

'Some of the time, yes, but I've also had a couple of spells in northern India—operating in the most basic conditions and with little help. If you think conditions are bad here you should see what they're like in some other parts of the world. We complain. They suffer in silence.'

Recalling her earlier belief that he did nothing that wouldn't further his own self-interest, she sought to clear her confused thoughts by asking, 'So why are you badgering me for more staff?'

'Simple. The more I have the opportunity to do at St Lukes, the more medical supplies I can make available for those in need in the Third World.'

Abbey experienced a suffocating tightening of her chest muscles as she recognised how unjust her unspoken criticism of him had been. 'You mean,' she asked, still breathless, 'all the money you earn with us is for others? I—I'd no idea.' She was finding it increasingly necessary to revise her opinion of the man she'd believed him to be.

He grinned self-consciously. 'I don't exactly know

why I'm telling you this. I didn't intend to for one moment. Few people know what I get up to in my periods of leave, and I prefer it that way.'

'I'm glad you've told me, Max.' She spoke quietly, still trying to come to terms with the fact that he was not the selfish person she had thought he was. 'It certainly sheds a different light on your demands at the hospital.'

He held up a dismissive hand. 'I don't want it to do that, Abbey. I certainly wasn't playing on your sympathy in an attempt to win you over. I—er—I suppose I thought it might help you to accept that our health service isn't as bad as it seems.'

Recognising that despite the outward trappings of the successful surgeon he was prepared to rough it when necessary, she said quietly, 'You must have seen some awful things.' She felt an intense surge of emotion as she recognised deep down that she hadn't been mistaken all those years ago. He really *was* the person she had thought him to be.

'I have, but I've also met some exceedingly hard-working and brave people—and I've enjoyed every moment of it.'

'Are you involved with a hospital over there?'

'Not exactly. A British charity has helped to kit out a train as a surgical unit. It's the only way to get help to people in some of the remoter districts where there are no roads. The train has three converted carriages—one is an operating theatre, one is living accommodation, labs and offices and the third carries essential supplies including a generator. The carriages are attached to a service train, and when we reach our intended destination they are uncoupled and shunted into specially cleared sidings.'

'I see. So you don't get that many turning up for treatment, then?'

'You must be joking. We get hundreds, and from miles away, too.'

Abbey was horrified. 'How do you cope?'

'It depends on what's available. At one place, we set a reception area up in one of the station buildings. Even that wasn't big enough, so we extended it with plastic sheeting and there we started the documentation and weeding out those we could help.'

'Surely you help them all?' Abbey was aghast.

'That would be impossible.'

'Then—then what about the others?'

Max shrugged. 'We do what we can. Sometimes it's only advice we can offer, but health education is a desperate need for most of them.'

'How do you manage that? With interpreters?'

'The intention is to use volunteer medics from each area we visit, then the majority will be able to speak the local dialects as well as English. It's worked so far.

'Many of the patients I've seen have deformities caused by an attack of polio, but surgery can't help them all. A lot more are given a better quality of life with calipers or crutches.'

'So is there a vaccination programme to prevent more cases in the future?'

'There is, but the decision to immunise has to be taken carefully.'

'Surely the more who are covered the better?'

Max shook his head. 'Not necessarily. Think about it. Live polio vaccine is the one that encourages the best compliance, but if it is given to just one child in a non-immune family, or, worse still, village, more harm than good is done. Especially when their sanitary arrangements leave much to be desired.'

'Of course! I can see what you mean now. That one child could start off an epidemic!' Abbey was thoughtful. 'How awful. I'd never thought about it that way.'

'You've never had to, that's all. Sure we get the occasional scare in this country, but the majority of us receive the vaccine as babies. But enough of my exploits.' He dismissed the subject as unimportant. 'We ought to be getting back—unless you've changed your mind, that is?' he asked with a provocative smile. 'Now you know what a thoroughly good guy I can be!'

She knew by the roguish twinkle in his eye that he didn't expect her to change her mind, but, bemused by what she'd been hearing and seduced by the wine and the warmth of the log fire, she was sorely tempted. However, aware that she would regret such a dangerous course of action, she shook her head and said firmly, as much for her own benefit as his, 'I really have to get back, Max.'

He grinned wryly. 'Probably just as well. You might be staying for the wrong reasons. And I very much doubt if I could promise to be a good guy all the time!'

He took hold of her hand as she rose from her chair, and led the way over to the cash desk. Having settled the bill, they collected her bag and made their way out to the car park. She shivered as the onslaught of razor-sharp cold air stripped her of the comforting warmth of the hotel.

Max wrapped a long arm around her waist and pulled her closer. 'Snuggle up and we'll both keep warm.'

Abbey was just beginning to enjoy the comforting contact with his body when he thrust her from him and gasped harshly, 'I don't believe it.'

'What's the matter, Max?'

'My car. Look. It's not there.'

Incongruously thinking that there was little point in her looking if it wasn't there, Abbey gazed around and saw that he was speaking the truth. Where the BMW had stood there was now a Mondeo.

'Are you sure you locked the car when you collected your bag?' he asked heatedly.

She pulled away from him angrily. 'Of course I'm sure. I'm not a fool.'

'I wasn't suggesting you were, but you could have made a mistake. There's no way anyone could have got in otherwise.'

'Don't you believe it,' she told him angrily. 'Dad always said if a professional thief decides he wants your car there's nothing you can do can stop him. And I can assure you I certainly locked it and heard the alarm setting as I walked away. Leaving a car unlocked is one thing my father taught me *never* to do.' She was so outraged that she started to move away from him.

'Perhaps things have changed since you dad's time in the force,' he muttered gruffly.

'Now you're suggesting I'm out of date.' Near to tears, their earlier rapport cruelly shattered, she voiced the accusation that was insistently forcing its way into her consciousness. 'I think you've done this deliberately.'

It was Max's turn to be angry. 'What on earth do you mean?'

'You arranged it so I'd have to spend the night with you and conveniently put the blame on me so I wouldn't suspect. I can read you too easily, Max Darby. You've softened me up with your tales of derring-do and—'

He shook his head in disbelief. 'Abbey, I can't believe you think I—you surely don't believe I'm that desperate? For goodness' sake, what do you think I am?'

Without waiting for an answer, he turned and strode towards the hotel entrance. 'Come inside and keep warm while I telephone the police,' he called over his shoulder.

It took much longer than Abbey expected for Max to get through. As the crime wasn't still in progress the hotel told Max not to dial 999, but gave him a special number for reporting crimes. By the time he had given the details twice to different officers, Abbey had calmed down sufficiently to realise that the BMW had genuinely been stolen and that Max was very upset about it. Her earlier accusation had been absurd. She couldn't imagine what had prompted her to make it. She supposed it must be due to her mixed-up emotions since he'd come back into her life.

'What now?' she asked him anxiously as he joined her on the wooden settle by the front door.

He shrugged miserably. 'Goodness knows. The police don't seem very hopeful. Or concerned. If they don't ring back within the next quarter of an hour, there's not much point in waiting.' He laughed grimly. 'At least it'll save me having the door replaced!'

Abbey had a sudden thought. 'Max, the hospital budget forecasts are in the boot!'

He shrugged. 'Let's hope it's a joyrider and not an industrial spy, then.'

His sarcasm was cutting, but she guessed she deserved it after what she'd said outside. 'How are we going to get home now?'

He shrugged. 'You tell me. Perhaps we'd better revise our plans after all. I'm sure the hotel will have rooms free at this time of year. Shall I go and find out?'

'I suppose so.' Abbey closed her eyes as she realised that the situation that she had tried to avoid now seemed inevitable. At least in a hotel like this towels and toiletries would be provided, so all she would need was her toothbrush! And in a single room it wouldn't matter that she had packed no nightwear!

She followed Max to the desk in time to hear, 'I'm sorry, sir. The only room we have left is a twin-bedded.'

CHAPTER SEVEN

MAX raised his eyebrows at Abbey and moved away from the desk. 'If that isn't Sod's Law!' he exclaimed. 'I suppose you think this is all part of my dastardly plan as well!'

Abbey shook her head. 'I shouldn't have said what I did earlier,' she confessed quietly.

'So, under the circumstances, would you object?'

She closed her eyes in mute appeal. 'Surely there's a taxi?' She was far from sure that she could trust herself in such close proximity to him.

'Probably, but it's a heck of a way and we could have a long wait. Especially on a Friday night. Surely we're both adult enough to accept that there's no alternative?'

Abbey wished she could be so certain! But, having already made a fool of herself by accusing him of setting the situation up deliberately, she could hardly now imply that she couldn't trust him. Or herself.

When she didn't answer, he whispered, 'I have seen it all before, you know, and it's not a double bed!'

Blushing furiously, Abbey reluctantly gave in. 'As long as you recognise I haven't changed my mind, and am only doing it for expediency's sake.'

'I'll be such a model of propriety, you won't recognise me!' He grinned before moving back to the reception desk and registering. Having collected the key, he asked for Room Service to send them up two large brandies before saying, once they were out of earshot of the night porter, 'At least your modesty will be covered. You've got your overnight bag. Mine's gone with the car!'

The realisation that she would now have to own up to its frugal contents—combined with finding herself in the situation that she had tried to avoid at all costs—suddenly struck Abbey as funny. She choked back a giggle as he opened the door to a comfortable room furnished in autumnal colours.

His frown told Abbey that he hadn't missed her amusement and was puzzled by it. However, he didn't comment, probably putting it down to embarrassment as he asked, 'Would you like to use the bathroom first?'

When she didn't answer, he said, 'Would you rather I went first and then buried my head under the bedclothes so I don't see you in your nightie?'

She couldn't continue the pretence any longer. She opened the bag and revealed its contents to him. 'This is what made me giggle. I had no intention of staying, Max. I put the toothbrush in for a joke.' When he didn't immediately speak, she said, 'You did ask where the fun-loving girl had gone!'

He joined in her laughter then and, encircling her with his long arms, kissed her lightly on the forehead. 'That was the reason! You were so quick collecting your overnight bag that I believed you must have had it packed ready and were protesting for the sake of it. And all the time. . .' His words tailed off as laughter overtook him again.

When he eventually regained control, he said quietly, 'It might be a good idea if we both stopped jumping to the wrong conclusions about each other.'

A knock on the door announced the arrival of their brandies. Abbey took the opportunity to move away from him and sit on the edge of one of the beds.

'I thought it would warm us both through.' He handed one of the glasses to Abbey. 'I think we're in the best place. It would be bitterly cold waiting for a taxi.'

When she didn't respond, he continued, 'Now, you

were were telling me about this unpacked bag. . .'

Sipping her drink thoughtfully, Abbey felt a sudden need to defend herself. 'You said a toothbrush, so that was what I brought!'

He moved over to sit beside her on the bed, slid his free arm round her waist and pulled her to him. 'Oh, Abbey, you haven't changed as much as you think. And I'm glad. Because I prefer the fun-to-be-with nurse I used to know to the hardened business executive you're trying to make yourself into.'

Panicking, Abbey tried to move away, but his hold tightened. 'You promised, Max.'

He nodded and gave her a comforting squeeze. 'I only promised not to do anything you didn't want me to. But I think you want this.' He leaned over and his lips met hers, the familiar musky scent of him arousing such a storm of remembered emotions that every vestige of her self-control crumbled, together with the front she'd been at such pains to keep up in his presence.

'Abbey, darling. This is more like it.' Between his repeated onslaught on her lips and her eager response, he murmured affectionate endearments in a way she clearly recalled him doing so often in the past.

When her body could take the increasing intimacy no longer without coming up for air, she placed her hands gently on his shoulders and, at her insistent pressure, he pulled slowly away.

He raised her chin with a finger and smiled into her eyes. 'I'm sure I'm not jumping to conclusions this time. You enjoyed that as much as I did.'

He searched for her lips again but, increasingly intimidated by the intensity of her feelings and the belief that he was merely playing with her affections, she opened her mouth to protest.

The words were never uttered. He seized the opportunity to invade the sensitive area beyond her lips with a gently probing tongue.

Despite her earlier apprehension, she couldn't resist the ache deep inside her urging her body into closer and closer contact with his. Encouraged, his hands strayed to shrug off the jacket of her business suit and then began to undo the top button of her blouse.

Suddenly aware that she was sliding headlong out of the control she was so desperate to retain, she somehow found the strength to resist.

She shouldn't have drunk the brandy. It was tricking her subconscious into believing that this was definitely where she belonged, when, in reality, she knew she didn't.

'No, Max, please. This is the reason I didn't want to stay.' At his gasp of disbelief, she murmured, 'I'm sorry, Max, but I mean it. This is wrong.' Her body's acute awareness of him belied every word she spoke, but if she allowed herself to be drawn into another casual affair she knew she would be the one left hurting at the end of it.

'Wrong? How can something so beautiful be wrong?' he uttered incredulously. 'I suppose you're going to tell me now that Ben's the only man in your life. Well, for those few moments your body told me otherwise. The way you just responded to me, I refuse to believe you're committed to him. Ben means nothing to you, does he? Your supposed relationship with him is just a useful buffer when something you can't handle threatens. I *thought* I might find out the truth this way.'

Incensed to discover that she'd been taken in by what now seemed obvious was merely an attempt to discover the strength of her feelings for Ben, she freed herself from his hold and snapped, 'How dare you criticise me, when you don't give a damn for anyone's feelings but your own?'

Max sighed deeply. 'Abbey, I'm not criticising, but

I do wonder what hold this fellow has over you. And I do care what the relationship is doing to your—'

Abbey interrupted him with a snort of derision. 'You expose my vulnerability and then say you care? You don't even know the meaning of the word. Everything has to be on your terms.'

Her anger was partly directed at herself—she'd been right to fear that she couldn't resist him. If nothing else, this episode had proved that she'd been wise to use Ben as a defence against Max's charisma, but it was obvious that it wasn't going to work in the future.

Especially now that Max had discovered that her body still responded to his lovemaking.

'You don't really believe that.'

'No?' If he had had even one genuine feeling for her, he would have known that she would feel used. No. It was clear now that his sole motive was to get what he wanted, when he wanted it, and in his own way. He wanted her in his power and would use any method to get her there.

'At least, if nothing else, it's shown me that I was right in not wanting to stay the night.'

He moved away slightly, disappointment evident in his every movement. 'Because you couldn't control me? Or because you couldn't control yourself?'

'Because it's happening ten years too late. Whatever you may think, Max, I have different needs from those you remember.' She made for the bathroom and, locking the door behind her, showered away the tears cascading down her cheeks.

Before emerging from the bathroom she splashed her face again with cold water. She slid into the nearest bed wearing only her cream satin teddy.

'Abbey—'

'I don't want to discuss it any more. I'm tired and I need to sleep.' She wanted him so badly but she wasn't prepared to resume a relationship that meant

so little to him. In any case, it wouldn't be fair on
Helen.

Max had made no pretence of averting his eyes as
she'd clambered into bed, and as he made his way to
the bathroom he shrugged ruefully. 'I honestly didn't
intend this to happen, Abbey.'

'Neither did I,' she snapped, 'so the sooner we forget
all about it the better.'

He sighed deeply as he made his way into the
bathroom.

She heard him splashing under the shower for what
seemed like hours. When he finally emerged he tried
to lighten the situation by saying, 'I won't kiss you
goodnight. I've lost my toothbrush!'

Abbey pretended to be asleep but watched through
narrowed lids as he stepped out of his trousers and
slipped beneath the duvet wearing only his underpants.
She did not respond to his murmured, 'Goodnight,
Abbey. Enjoy sweet dreams because you're safe with
me. I keep my promises.'

Keeps his promises, she thought scathingly. Like he
was going to ring her the moment he was settled. Like
he wouldn't do anything she didn't want him to.
Although if the vivid memory of his kiss was anything
to go by she had to admit that she *had* wanted it. And
he'd known it.

Wide awake now, she lay stiffly, her mind in over-
drive as she relived the events of the evening. She
listened to Max's regular breathing, afraid to move lest
she should wake him, and wished that she could be
wrong about him.

Surely there was no way that someone who could
care so devotedly for people on the other side of the
world would have cruelly abandoned her without a
word? And yet what else could she believe? Her
thoughts chased round and round in her head, but she
came to no conclusion. Her last waking thought was

to wonder miserably if in some way she had been partly
to blame.

Abbey woke to the sound of Max moving quietly
around the room. Seeing she was awake, he brought
her a cup of tea and perched on the side of her bed
as if their disagreement had never happened.

'It's a sparkling morning at the moment, but the sun
is rapidly banishing the frost. Stay where you are.
I'm going down to see if there's any news of my car.
Continental breakfast in bed?'

She nodded. 'Sounds nice, if that's all right by you.
Or would you prefer a cooked breakfast?'

He patted his firm waistline. 'No fear. I'll
organise it.'

The moment the door closed behind him, Abbey
slipped out of bed and into the bathroom. By the time
he returned, she was dressed and seated in front of
the window.

'I thought you were having breakfast in bed?'

'I changed my mind. The view from this window is
unbelievable.'

He came and sat beside her, first leaning over to
kiss her cheek. 'Still not trust me?'

She looked suitably abashed but breakfast arrived
at that moment, preventing the need for a reply.

'That smells good.' He placed the tray on the window
table and uncovered breakfast with a flourish. 'And,
by gosh, it looks good.'

When the coffee was poured, she asked, 'What news
of the car?'

Max shook his head. 'Nothing. It's disappeared without a trace, apparently. The hotel are arranging for
me to hire one. Obviously I can't be without.'

'You could borrow mine if we can get back to
Bleasdon.'

'That's very generous of you, but I couldn't possibly

deprive the hospital manager of her official transport,' he mocked gently, 'even if she does only work office hours!'

Angry spots of colour highlighted her cheeks. 'That's hardly fair when I have to attend your MedCom meetings and others in the evening, not to mention frequently being on call should there be any problems at St Luke's. My hours are no more regular than when I was nursing.'

'But you expected them to be?' He didn't hide the surprise in his voice. 'You're still not comfortable with your managerial position, are you?' He lazily selected a croissant and sliced it through the centre.

Abbey watched his precise movements. 'Not when you're around,' she confessed, trying desperately to ignore the intimacy of their shared meal.

'So what are your plans for the remainder of the weekend?'

'If there are no problems awaiting me at the hospital, I shall restock my larder. And if your car isn't found I'll have to redo all the figures that were in my file.'

'I shouldn't be too hasty. They might turn up.'

She raised her head sharply, wondering if, after all, he knew something about the car that she didn't, but, meeting his gaze, she found no sign of subterfuge there.

'And tomorrow?' he pressed. 'What will you do tomorrow?'

'Probably meet up with friends.'

'Friends?' he queried suggestively and she knew he was probing to discover if it was Ben.

'Don't you think I have any?' she retorted, deliberately misunderstanding.

'I'd guess you have plenty—but it's that special someone in your life I'm no longer sure about.'

Abbey lowered her eyes and carefully picked out a

croissant. She pointedly concentrated on eating it rather than saying something she might later wish she hadn't.

'You don't want to talk about him? Regretting your response to me last night, perhaps?'

When she again didn't answer, he leaned across the table and ran his finger down her cheek. 'Methinks the lady doesn't protest enough.'

'You're not so hot on Shakespeare as you are on the Bible,' she snapped.

Max grinned maddeningly. 'I could hardly say you protested too much when you won't speak to me!'

She glared at him before returning her concentration to the croissant. 'My private life has absolutely nothing to do with you. You forfeited that right many years ago.'

'So you keep telling me.' He spoke quietly, but when she raised her eyes to search his face his expression spoke volumes.

She recognised that her attempt to distance herself from him was having the opposite effect, and her heart lurched painfully. She didn't know whether to be pleased or disappointed when they were interrupted by the harsh jangle of the telephone.

He snatched up the receiver, obviously annoyed by the interruption.

'Yes?' He listened intently for a few moments, then answered, 'I'll come down.'

This didn't appear to please the person on the other end, so, after another lengthy tirade, he muttered, 'OK. You'd better send him up.'

He replaced the receiver. 'It's the police. In uniform. It's bad for the hotel's image if I meet him in Reception.'

She nodded and, draining her coffee-cup, said, 'I'll make myself scarce.'

He glowered at her. 'Why on earth should you?

We're far enough away from Bleasdon for it not to affect your reputation.'

'That wasn't what I meant,' she responded quietly.

'Are you sure? That seems to be all you care about these days.'

Jolted by the injured tone of his voice, she retorted, 'You know that's not true—'

'Do I?' he broke in. 'How?' She guessed he was referring to her refusal to take the flowers with them on Friday and her worry about them arriving at the hospital together after the meal at Melissa's.

How unjust when she'd done it as much for his reputation as hers. She was prevented from saying so by the arrival of the policeman.

He took down a myriad of details but could offer little hope of Max getting his car back. 'I shouldn't think it was a joyrider, sir. Cars like yours are taken for a market and it's probably been sold on by now.'

Hearing her own theory confirmed, Abbey resisted the temptation to say 'I told you so', but Max's expression as he glanced at her told her that he was only too well aware of her thoughts.

'I need a replacement for work as soon as possible so I can tell my insurance company that, can I?'

The constable looked uncomfortable. 'We can't be sure, sir. I'm just voicing my opinion. I only called by because the hotel manager insisted. If we do find it, we'll let you know immediately.'

He made his escape as fast as he could. Max shook his head as he closed the door behind him and said brusquely, 'Why did they bother?' He shrugged hopelessly. 'I must get back and see my insurance company before they close this morning. The hire car should have arrived by now, so we'll leave when you're ready.'

Suddenly aware that his attitude towards her had changed, Abbey hastily cleaned her teeth and threw her brush back into her overnight bag. 'I'm packed,' she said with a smile to try and lift the morose mood that had suddenly descended on Max.

He didn't acknowledge her attempted humour and, recognising how her lack of trust had hurt him, she couldn't really blame him for not wasting any more time trying to reason with her.

He signed the forms for the hire car at the reception desk and, having settled their bill, carried her bag out to the dark red Astra pointed out to them.

Hardly speaking, he drove straight to St Luke's and round to the car park. Lifting her bag from his car, he dropped it into the boot of her Fiesta and said derisively, 'I won't shake hands—someone might be watching.'

'Max. . .' Wanting to let him know that, despite how it must seem, she *did* value his friendship and support, Abbey started to thank him, intending to try and explain her cautious attitude. But all she could do was watch helplessly as, ignoring her, he climbed into the driving seat and drove away without a backward glance.

Her heart sank painfully in her chest as she realised the damage she had done. Hadn't he fought to keep Tom Renny from taking his patients elsewhere? Made sure that the other two surgeons would return their business from the Cotswold once she had sorted the staffing situation at St Lukes?

Wondering what else he had done that she didn't know about, she was suddenly ashamed that she'd been too busy protecting her personal feelings to appreciate his subtle support as chairman of the MedCom. Support for her position that might well not be on offer any longer after the way she'd behaved.

Although surely he must understand her reluctance to become personally involved a second time. Was that why he had sent her flowers? On Valentine's Day of all days? Thoroughly confused, she shook her head miserably.

'I thought you were coming back last night.' The security officer's voice behind her made her jump and, recognising the insinuation, she saw that he too had watched Max drive out of the grounds.

'Mr Darby's car was stolen, so they gave us beds at the Mercy.' It was the first thing she thought of to try and allay his suspicion.

As she walked across to the hospital, she crossed her fingers at the white lie. Perhaps Max was right. Was her worry about her reputation making her start to behave stupidly?

'Morning, Miss Westray,' the receptionist greeted her.

'Good morning,' Abbey smiled. 'Any mail for me?'

The girl checked and handed her a couple of envelopes.

Abbey made her way up to her office and unlocked her door. Jane had left some papers on her desk and Abbey slit open the two envelopes she'd been given and placed their contents on top.

Slipping out of her jacket, she was about to hang it up when she saw that Jane had returned the roses to her window-sill.

'Silly girl,' she muttered to herself. 'Why didn't she take them home?'

She switched on her coffee-machine and settled down to work through the pile of papers on her desk. But her mind was only half on what she was reading. Her thoughts were preoccupied with the white lie she'd told the security man.

Supposing someone mentioned it in conversation to Max and he showed surprise? It really would look as if they had something to hide!

She ought to tell him what she'd said, and sooner

rather than later. But she couldn't just ring and tell him. Not after the way he'd already accused her of being over-protective of her reputation.

The problem refused to be ignored so it was a relief to discover that only one item amongst all the papers she scanned needed immediate attention. It was an accident form filled in by Helen, stating that an agency nurse had injured her back by not using the lifting equipment provided.

Abbey sighed and made her way down to the operating theatres. 'How did it happen, Helen?'

'It was quite late yesterday evening. I was scrubbed in the other theatre. She apparently said she didn't know how to use the lifting frame, and wouldn't wait to be taught. She asked the anaesthetist to help her lift a neuro patient. I think she probably just pulled a muscle.'

'Was she seen by anyone?'

'No. She insisted she would be OK.'

Abbey rang the girl and discovered that she was at home, unable to work as her back was so painful.

'Have you seen a doctor?' Abbey asked her, conscious that the girl was losing money because of an injury sustained at St Luke's.

'No. If it's no better I'll get an appointment on Monday.'

'Would you like me to arrange for one of our consultants to call?'

The agency nurse seemed surprised by the offer but accepted gratefully. 'Thank you. I'd appreciate that.'

Abbey returned to her office, aware that she'd made the offer partly in case the nurse should make a claim against St Luke's and partly so that she had an excuse to ring Max. She sat looking at the telephone for several minutes before lifting the receiver and asking the receptionist to bleep him.

When the telephone rang several moments later, she

lifted the receiver to hear Max's amused voice enquire, 'Can't manage without me after all?'

'No. Well, yes, I suppose so. In a way.'

'I see,' he responded tersely. 'You'd better tell me in what way, then. And quickly. I've a couple of patients waiting for me to say if they can go home.'

She told him about the agency nurse. 'So I wondered if you would do a home consultation. See if she needs treatment. The hospital budget will cover the cost of your visit and anything that needs to be done.'

He didn't reply immediately and she wondered if she had offended him by offering money.

'What's her name and address?' She heard the question with relief and gave him the details.

'I'll get over there before lunch. Will you still be at the hospital?'

'I've plenty of paperwork to be going on with—I'll wait to hear from you. Thanks. Oh! And Max?'

'Yes?' he queried suspiciously.

'I'm afraid I told a white lie earlier. I—I told the security man here they'd given us beds at the Mercy when your car was stolen. I hope you don't mind telling the same story.'

She heard the amusement in his voice as he told her, 'If you expect that to stop the rumours you're mistaken. You'd have been better to say nothing.'

'It was the security man—I wasn't prepared. He must have watched you drive off and came straight over, asking why I hadn't come back yesterday evening as I'd said I would.'

His amusement increased. 'If you'd done as I suggested in the first place and told everyone you wouldn't be back, there'd have been no problem.'

'But I didn't think it was a good idea and I was right, wasn't I?'

Ignoring her query, he said softly, 'So, you want me to say we had separate rooms at the Mercy? I think

I could manage that. But only if you do something for me.'

'What's that?' Abbey asked dubiously.

'I'll let you know when I've seen this bad back.'

CHAPTER EIGHT

THE telephone rang again almost the moment Abbey replaced the receiver. She lifted it to hear the nurse in charge of the ward that afternoon asking for permission to call in a bank nurse later if necessary.

'What's the problem?' Abbey asked.

'One of Mr Darby's patients isn't too well and if she goes on this way I may need to leave someone with her all the time. I thought I'd ask while you were on the premises rather than disturb you later at home.'

'Which patient?' Abbey asked.

'Mrs Jenkins. She isn't helping herself at all. In fact she seems to have given up.'

'I'm waiting for a phone call at the moment. I'll come and see her afterwards. However, if you need to get another nurse in that's fine.'

Max returned her call within the hour. 'I've seen your theatre nurse. I don't think it's anything dramatic. I've given her a prescription for drugs to reduce the inflammation and told her to rest flat for three days. If it's no better then, we'll get an X-ray done.'

'You don't think one's necessary at the moment?'

'No. Definitely not. It would be exposing her to X-rays unnecessarily and that's the last thing I want to do.'

'I wouldn't expect you to, Max. I'll keep in touch with her and let you know if she needs to be seen again.'

'I've already arranged a time for her to come and see me on Tuesday. If she isn't feeling any better she'll contact my secretary.'

'I see. Perhaps you'd let me know what's happening.

If she's off work for more than three days as a result of the accident we have to report it to the health and safety executive.'

'No problem.'

'I'm very grateful, Max.'

'I shouldn't be too complacent,' he warned. 'If you're not to end up paying compensation to someone who's injured themselves at *your* hospital, you'll have to find a way to ensure that the bank and agency nurses are trained in using any equipment that's provided to help them.'

Abbey sighed. 'I know, but it's not easy. Most of those involved have other commitments that prevent them coming in apart from the times they work. I know Helen has tried in the past but that won't be good enough in the eyes of the law. I'll talk to her about it again on Monday.'

'Good. Now that's settled, perhaps we can discuss my condition for confirming your story about where we stayed.'

'Which is?'

'I've been thinking over what happened last night and I feel we should meet up somewhere neutral and, over a meal, try to clear up some of the misconceptions we both appear to be harbouring. Somewhere local this time. A repeat of last night's events is the last thing we need.'

Unsure as to exactly which events he was objecting to, Abbey demurred. 'I'm not sure. You see—'

'Abbey. I have more than enough work to do. You have a similar workload. It would be easier for both of us if we could work together rather than continue to pull in opposing directions.'

If that was all he wanted to discuss, even though the dangers were obvious, it was a risk she was now prepared to take. 'When do you suggest?'

'Can you manage this evening?'

'I suppose so.'

'Don't sound so enthusiastic.'

'Sorry, Max. It's just that I've lots to do. I've come back to a pile of papers and want to get everything sorted out if I can. Also, I think I may need to find more staff for the ward. Your patient, Mrs Jenkins, sounds as if she needs extra attention. I'm on my way down to see her now and find out how they're managing.'

'I was coming in to see her later. What's the problem?'

'Just her general condition giving cause for concern, I think. The RMO is keeping an eye on her.'

'Is it Ellie Wycliffe on call?'

'Yes. She's on for the weekend.'

'That's OK, then. I'd trust her with my mother. I'll see you later and we can make an arrangement then.'

'OK,' Abbey agreed, replacing her receiver. But she couldn't ignore the shaft of jealousy once again piercing her heart as she recalled the attention he had paid Ellie at that first MedCom meeting. Goodness, she told herself sternly. If you're going to feel this way about every female Max comes into contact with, isn't your heart trying to tell you something?

She made her way thoughtfully down to the ward level. 'How's it going?' she asked the senior nurse who had rung her earlier.

The pretty brunette smiled. 'Just about coping.'

'Have you enough staff for the rest of the weekend?' Abbey ran her finger down the duty rota on the wall.

'It really depends on whether Mrs Jenkins continues to go downhill.'

Abbey nodded as she turned to leave the office. 'I'll go and take a look at her.'

Two nurses were in the process of turning Mrs Jenkins, and Abbey read through the case notes whilst she waited for them to finish.

When their patient was comfortable, they left Abbey with her. 'Ring the bell if you want anything,' one of them told her.

Abbey seated herself by the bed and took hold of one of the frail hands that were plucking at the bedcovers. 'Hello, Mrs Jenkins. How are you feeling?'

'About the same. The nurses do what they can.'

'Is there anything else we can do to make you more comfortable?' Abbey asked.

Mrs Jenkins nodded silently before saying, 'Let me go. I don't like it here.'

Abbey patted her hand reassuringly. 'We'll let you go home as soon as you can cope and we can find you some help. In the meantime we'll do what we can to help.'

'There's no one at home. I live all alone.'

'I know. That's why we don't want you to go back there yet.'

The elderly face crumpled as Mrs Jenkins muttered vehemently, 'I don't want to go back.'

Abbey tried to calm her patient by gently smoothing the hair back from her forehead. 'Don't worry about it at the moment. We'll no doubt find something suitable when the time comes.'

'I don't want you to. Just leave me to die. I've nothing to live for.'

Abbey lifted a tissue from the box on the locker and gently wiped away the tears that were cascading down her patient's cheeks. 'You've been through a difficult time, Mrs Jenkins. I'm sure you'll soon feel differently.'

She shook her head. 'I won't. I've had enough.'

Abbey squeezed the frail hand gently. 'Even so, it's our job to keep you as comfortable as possible so tell us if there's anything you need.'

Opening her eyes wide, Mrs Jenkins gave Abbey a weak smile. '*You* know what I mean. I can tell. Not like those doctors who must save life at any cost. Or the young nurses—they don't understand.'

'Yes, I understand,' Abbey reassured her quietly, feeling like Methuselah.

Mrs Jenkins drifted in and out of sleep, but Abbey stayed at her side until her hand was released by the sleeping woman.

After waiting to see if she stirred again, Abbey made her way to the ward office.

'Poor Mrs Jenkins seems to have lost the will to live,' she told the charge nurse now seated at the ward desk.

'She hasn't got much going for her, has she? No relatives that she's told us about, and she says all her friends have died before her.'

Abbey nodded. 'I know. She needs lots of loving care.'

'We're doing all we can, but she's definitely not as well as she was yesterday.'

'I can see that. She's sleeping peacefully at the moment. If you're at all worried, or there's anything you need, I can be reached on my bleeper.'

The pretty nurse nodded gratefully. 'If she gets to the stage where she can't be left we definitely won't have enough staff, especially tomorrow.'

'Let me know immediately if that happens. You can bleep me any time, but I'll be in my office for the next couple of hours. Oh—and if Mr Darby comes in to see her while I'm still around I'd like to see him.'

It was nearly an hour later that Max knocked on her door. 'I got your message. Another problem?'

'Oh—er—yes.' Abbey was flustered. 'I wanted to see you about Mrs Jenkins.' He leaned across her desk and kissed her with lips that barely touched her forehead, but which nonetheless sent a surging warmth through her blood.

Watching her confusion, his dark eyes glimmered

with amusement as he pulled up a chair and waited expectantly.

'I had a chat with her earlier and feel you ought to know she's losing the will to live.'

'So the ward staff tell me.'

He waited for her to add to the information he already possessed.

'I think she would prefer it if you didn't intervene if her condition deteriorates.'

'You mean no resuscitation?'

'She said you doctors save lives at all costs, and that the young nurses don't understand either.' Abbey smiled. 'She seemed to suggest that as I was so much older I would understand.'

Max raised a surprised eyebrow. 'Message about Mrs Jenkins received and understood.' He smiled then, a teasing smile that had an unsettling effect on her composure. 'Now, we'd better arrange our meal before you need a Bath chair to get to it! I'll pick you up at seven-fifteen. OK?'

Abbey lifted her eyes to search his face and saw a gentleness in his expression that made her grateful that he was disegarding her earlier reluctance. 'I'll look forward to that.'

He grinned approvingly. 'Praise be. Progress at last. See you later, then.' He repeated the butterfly touch of his lips on her cheek and was gone.

When he'd left, Abbey checked her watch and, discovering that it was nearly four-thirty, decided to call it a day. Collecting the bare minimum of groceries on her way, she was back at her flat in plenty of time for a luxurious bath.

Remembering the last time that Max had collected her there, she was ready early. She dressed appropriately for a pub meal—black trousers and jacket with a cream silk blouse. However, just after seven the telephone rang.

'Hi, Abbey. I'm awfully sorry but I'm going to have to break our arrangement.'

Arrangement? Not date? Abbey thought miserably. Was that all this meeting had meant to him after all? Had she misread his earlier vibes? Bemused, she could think of nothing to say but, 'OK.'

'Sorry not to have given you more notice, but it was an away match and after being examined at the local A and E he's only just arrived on my doorstep.'

'Who's "he"?'

'Denny Dale. You remember. The arthroscopy you helped me with. Silly lad didn't listen to either of us and played again today when he wasn't match-fit and he's really done in his cartilage this time. I'm taking him to Theatre almost immediately. He's already admitted to St Luke's.'

'Would you like me to come over and scrub?' She asked the question tentatively.

'No, thanks. Helen's here. And Ellie will assist.'

'That's good.' Abbey couldn't think of anything else to say. She'd been about to offer him a meal when he finished, but she wasn't prepared to do so when he already had his harem with him. 'Hope it goes all right. I'll see you Monday, then.'

She replaced the receiver without giving him a chance to say otherwise. Why, oh, why, when they were thrown together at the hotel, hadn't she seized the opportunity offered to her? Her behaviour last night had been enough to drive him into the arms of every female who showed even the tiniest interest. She went through to her bedroom and replaced the blouse and jacket with a T-shirt. She thought about changing into her jeans, but her disappointment was so great that the effort was just too much trouble.

She couldn't be bothered to cook anything for herself either so, despite having eaten nothing since the hotel breakfast, she settled in front of the TV with a sandwich.

She must have drifted off to sleep almost immediately as she woke at eleven to find half the sandwich uneaten. It was no wonder she was tired. She'd had little enough sleep the night before and her dealings with Max were leaving her emotionally exhausted. Perhaps after a good night's sleep she would see things differently.

Penny was in charge of the ward on Sunday. She rang Abbey at home. 'I'm sorry to disturb you, Miss Westray, but Mr Darby's patient needs someone with her all the time and I just don't have enough staff.'

'Mrs Jenkins, you mean?'

'That's right. I've contacted all our bank staff and not one of them can help. It's too short notice. I wonder if you'd give permission for an agency nurse for one day?'

Abbey thought rapidly. Agency nurses were far from cheap, especially on a Sunday. For this reason her predecessor had banned them. But this was an emergency.

'Perhaps we can make an exception this time,' she agreed, then, remembering the distressed nonagenarian she had chatted with the day before, she changed her mind. There was no way she could abandon her to the unknown capability of an agency nurse. 'On second thoughts, I'll come in and sit with her myself.'

'Are you sure?' Penny sounded as if she didn't believe Abbey could possibly mean it.

'Quite sure. She needs someone she knows. Not a stranger.'

'I suppose she does.' The sister seemed surprised that Abbey should even consider the patient's needs.

'I can stay today as long as necessary, but perhaps you can have a bank nurse on stand-by for tomorrow.'

'I have my doubts whether she'll last that long but

I can't tell, obviously. There are enough night staff to cope, so you won't be needed after nine.'

'That's fine by me. I'll be in directly.'

Abbey quietly entered the patient's room, and smiled to let the care assistant seated beside the bed know that she was relieved.

The old lady's eyes flickered, but she didn't speak.

Abbey heard footsteps behind her and turned to find Max and Ellie in the doorway. The resident medical officer was describing the deterioration in Mrs Jenkins's condition.

'Right, I'll take a look.'

Ellie hovered while Abbey helped Max to examine the patient. As he listened to her chest, he raised his eyes to meet Abbey's and almost imperceptibly shook his head.

'She's no relatives, has she?' he asked at length.

'No. A neighbour keeps an eye on her.'

Max nodded.

When he'd finished writing on the notes, Abbey asked, 'Have you seen anything of Andy? I wondered how he was.'

'Much better, thanks. The injury has turned out to be less serious than I thought.'

'That's good. And how's your footballer?'

'Bounding with energy. He's already trying to do too much too soon. However, the physio will hopefully put a stop to that. She's with him now, so I'll go and see how she's getting on.'

He left Abbey seated by Mrs Jenkins. She moistened the patient's lips and stroked her hair back from her forehead.

The care assistant returned almost immediately. 'Mr Darby wants to see you in the office. I'll stay here.'

*   *   *

'Have you seen the physio?'

'She'll come along here when she leaves Denny. It's Mrs Jenkins I wanted to see you about. I'm afraid she's not going to make it,' he told Abbey the moment she had closed the office door behind her.

She nodded. 'I gathered that. Is there anything we can do to make her more comfortable?'

He shook his head. 'We've done everything possible. If her condition had been better before the fall it might have been different, but her neighbour tells me she didn't bother to eat and refused all offers of help. Even for her sister.'

'Her sister?'

He nodded. 'Bedridden. For many years. The only people Mrs Jenkins let into the house were two district nurses who washed her sister each day. The powers that be asked the nurses to do what they could, but Mrs Jenkins was staunchly independent. That type of person makes it difficult to do anything to help.'

'When did her sister die?'

He grimaced wryly. 'It doesn't take much to work it out, does it? A month ago. Mrs J. had already lost the will to live when she had the fall.'

Abbey felt a deep compassion for the old lady, alone in the foreign surroundings of the hospital. She'd obviously fought to keep her sister at home where she belonged, and there was no one to do the same for her. She must hate her loss of independence. No wonder she didn't want to go on living.

'She needs lots of TLC, and that we can give her,' Abbey said.

'Not too much intrusion, though. Just keep her comfortable. Perhaps you'd explain that to whoever is going to remain with her.'

'I am.'

Max raised his eyebrows quizzically. 'I thought you said you weren't missing the nursing side of things.'

'I'm not,' she defended hotly. 'I'm doing this for Mrs Jenkins—and in the interest of cutting costs!'

'I'll believe you, thousands wouldn't.' He grinned.

'*You* wouldn't,' she retorted, 'but I understand how she feels. Not everyone would. And I see this as one of the advantages of working in a smaller place—it means I get the best of both worlds.' She surprised herself by the vehemence of her defence, but she had to admit that she was enjoying having sole responsibility for a patient again.

'If you say so. I'm not so sure, but now isn't the right time to debate the issue. How about supper when you finish here?'

Annoyed by his obvious scepticism and his lack of concern at breaking their 'arrangement' the evening before, Abbey demurred. 'I don't know. I'll be here until nine and I seem to have lost most of my weekend one way or another.'

'OK.' He shrugged. 'I'll pop back later, then, to see how she is. I want to keep an eye on Denny as well.'

He'd certainly called her bluff by not trying to change her mind, but it was too late to do anything about it. She made her way slowly to Mrs Jenkins's room, aware that she was fooling herself if she thought she could gauge his reaction to any given situation. He was, as she'd discovered time and time again, unpredictable. Dismissing her personal thoughts to the back of her mind, Abbey indicated to the young girl that she was ready to take charge of the patient again.

'Can I get you anything?' the care assistant asked, obviously delighted to be relieved once again of what she considered a boring chore.

'No, thanks.' Abbey smiled. 'How long have you worked here?' She read the girl's name-badge. 'Myra, is it?'

The girl nodded. 'I've been here nearly seven months,' she answered nervously.

'Are you enjoying it?'

'Yes, thank you. And I'm learning ever such a lot.'

Abbey smiled her approval. 'That's good to hear.'

As the girl left the room, Abbey picked up Mrs Jenkins's charts to discover what medication was necessary and when. She seated herself quietly by the side of the bed to study them.

The patient opened her eyes and, appearing to note the change of nurse, mumbled incoherently.

Abbey took her hand. 'I'll be here if you want anything.'

The drooping eyes closed again. 'Nothing to live for.'

Startled by the sudden clarity of her words, repeating what she had said the day before, Abbey said quietly, 'Once we get you walking properly—'

'No point,' muttered Mrs Jenkins. 'No one to care for or to care about me.'

'We care. And Mr Darby cares.'

The old lady gave an almost imperceptible shake of her head and repeated her earlier words. 'Nothing to live for. I want to go to Bessie.' She rested back on her pillow and her mouth fell open, allowing an unnatural snore to escape.

Abbey released her hand and pushed the door closed to prevent neighbouring patients from being disturbed.

Mrs Jenkins continued to snore, but her words left disturbing thoughts to tumble through Abbey's mind.

'No one to care for or to care about me' could equally apply to her. As Max had said, she'd been close to her father—much more so than she had ever been to her mother—and though she had plenty of friends there was no one special in her life.

After her brief fling with Max, she'd opted for independence as a way of never being hurt again.

Had she really become as hard as Max had suggested? Was he merely trying to rescue her before it was too late?

Suddenly she wasn't sure of anything. Even what she wanted from life!

Through the long afternoon she debated the pros and cons with herself until she knew without doubt that she wanted something more. If she was honest with herself she had to admit that, having achieved her ambition of becoming a hospital manager, she would happily abandon it to share her life with Mr Right should he appear on the horizon.

And although she longed for it to be Max she was certain that, however strong her feelings were for him, they weren't reciprocated. Sure, he found her a challenge, but he obviously enjoyed his single status more.

Mrs Jenkins stirred again, running her dry tongue round her mouth. Abbey gently moistened her lips, only too happy to abandon her introspection to the more important task of looking after her patient.

She repeatedly checked Mrs Jenkins's pulse and blood pressure and over the afternoon detected a steady decline in her condition. Max had said that he would be in to see her later, but Abbey began to doubt if he would find her alive.

She experienced a growing empathy with Mrs Jenkins, understanding exactly how the patient felt. She'd had a long life and didn't want to continue living. She was comfortable and pain-free and, knowing that Abbey was beside her, secure.

The young nursing assistant brought Abbey a cup of tea after a while and asked if she wanted a break away from her task, but Abbey refused. She was enjoying doing something practical, and was happy to stay where she was.

Max came at seven. 'How's she doing?' he whispered.

Abbey shook her head and silently handed him the charts.

After checking his patient's pulse, he helped Abbey

to turn Mrs Jenkins and make her comfortable. Then he settled down quietly beside Abbey. His presence gave her a sudden sense of togetherness that she hoped might continue when she returned to her management duties.

As she turned to smile at him their silent rapport was dashed by his bleeper going off.

After answering the call in the ward office, he popped his head round the door and told her briefly, 'Sorry to desert you but I've a patient to see at the General.'

When he'd gone, Abbey moistened Mrs Jenkins's lips again and sponged her face before settling down beside her once more.

Accompanied by Ellie, Max came back an hour or so later—but only in response to Abbey's call for the resident medic.

Abbey turned as they came into the room. 'I'm afraid you're too late,' she told them quietly.

Max nodded. 'I rather expected as much. I'm sorry not to have been back earlier, Abbey. Are you all right?'

'Fine,' she answered brusquely, choking back the threatening tears that were not only for Mrs Jenkins but also for herself.

He moved closer and, putting a hand on her arm, asked, 'Are you sure? You've not had much practice at coping with death recently.'

'Of course I'm sure. I'm just sad that she died with no one else to care.'

Ellie looked up from checking Mrs Jenkins's vital signs. 'She didn't want to go on living, you know.'

Abbey glared at her furiously. 'I know exactly how she felt.'

Ellie ignored her hostility. 'For your records, I certified death at 20.14 hours.' She noted the time herself.

Gently pulling the sheet over Mrs Jenkins's face,

Abbey turned to complete her records, and when she'd finished, picked up all the papers and strode out of the room to find Penny.

'Thanks for all you've done, Miss Westray. We can manage now. Sorry to have ruined your weekend.'

'No problem. I'm glad I was able to do what I could for her. I do wonder, though, what happened to her husband. The only person she seemed to miss was her sister.'

'Apparently he was lost during the First World War. They married young and luckily or unluckily, depending on how you look at it, had no children before he was drafted.'

'That's sad. It happened to so many.'

Penny nodded. 'It makes you realise the importance of snatching any moment of happiness as it arises.'

Abbey heard her words with a sinking heart. Perhaps all along she had been looking for too much in the way of commitment from Max. She should have done exactly what Penny suggested and snatched her happiness while she could.

She looked up to see Max steering Ellie towards the lift, a comforting hand under her elbow. 'I shouldn't be long,' he told her, turning back towards Abbey.

Aware of her wildly swinging emotions, she knew she had to get away before she made a fool of herself.

'Coming to the canteen?'

So that was where Ellie was waiting. 'I've a couple of things to do here, then I must get home.'

'You need to eat.'

She needed time to sort herself out more. 'I will, when I get home.'

Max gave her a long and studied look.

Abbey tried to make excuses. 'If you remember, I lost all the papers I took to the Mercy. I need to redo them.'

Max sighed deeply. 'And it's all my fault, I suppose.

If I hadn't suggested a meal on Friday you'd still have your precious figures, and if I'd looked after my patient better you wouldn't have been needed in here today.'

'Of course it's not your fault,' she told him snappily, immediately regretting her outburst and yet unable to control it. 'Mrs Jenkins might have been your patient but she was also one of mine. I'm in charge of the hospital and I wanted to stay with her. And now I'm going home.'

Abbey knew she was being irrational but she couldn't help herself. Max seemed to have the ability to confuse her until she said all the things she hadn't intended to and certainly didn't mean.

She stormed up to her office, collected the papers she needed to work on, drove home, and sat up half the night.

She spent so much time berating herself for her stupidity that everything took much longer than it should have done. As she made her way to bed, she knew things couldn't go on the way they were. Whilst she undressed, she spoke to her reflection in the mirror.

'It's up to you, my girl. Why should Max make a commitment to you, any more than he seems prepared to with Helen or Ellie? And can you possibly expect him to offer anything more than you had before when you keep him at arm's length all the time?'

The solution was in her own hands. Before it was too late she must ditch, once and for all, her pretence of a relationship with Ben and then work at making herself indispensable in Max's life. If they only ever crossed swords at work, how would he ever recognise what he was missing?

Relieved at having come to what was probably her first sensible decision where Max was concerned, Abbey washed, got into bed, and immediately fell into a deep and restful sleep.

CHAPTER NINE

WHEN Abbey awoke at the alarm's buzz, she was surprised to find that she had slept. But although she was at her desk on time she felt nothing like work.

However, her mood improved considerably when she discovered that Jane had collected together several applications from theatre-trained staff.

Having looked through them carefully, she picked out several who she decided would be useful to the hospital.

She rang through to the operating theatre and asked Helen to come up and discuss the feasibility of taking one of them on contract.

'We can't go mad, but with another scrub nurse you should be able to gradually increase the number of day cases and then, hopefully, with the income from these we can employ more ward nurses. That would let us tackle more long-stay cases.'

Obviously pleased, Helen said, 'Max will be delighted. He's forever saying that's what we should be doing.'

'I've been made only too aware of his feelings on the subject,' Abbey told her coolly.

Recognising Abbey's lack of enthusiasm, Helen rushed to his defence. 'He doesn't want the money he earns here for himself, you know. He uses it to help people abroad who have no medical care.'

'I've been made well aware of that as well,' Abbey told her grimly, 'and I'm glad if my actions make a contribution in that direction. However, my first priority is to get the hospital on a sound financial basis. Any other benefits are secondary.'

'Oh, yes, I realise that. I didn't mean—'

'I know you didn't, Helen.' Realising that her personal feelings were colouring her attitude towards the theatre sister, Abbey sought to make amends. 'These haven't been the easiest few weeks of my life, but I feel I'm getting on top of things now. Unless the medics start clamouring for more changes.'

'I shouldn't think they'd do that,' Helen assured her.

'Not this week, anyway,' Abbey agreed wryly. 'But I don't underestimate them!'

'What made you give up theatre work and move into management?'

Unwilling to divulge the truth about her broken relationship, Abbey shrugged. 'Many reasons, I suppose.'

'Max seems to understand why you're doing it, but even he thinks you're hiding your talents under a bushel.'

Abbey couldn't help smiling. 'In that case, he's mixing his biblical quotes!' Seeing Helen's look of incomprehension, she added, 'I'm being pedantic. It's just more usual to hide your light under a bushel. What I'm really trying to say is that you know as well as I do that the only way for a nurse to get near the top of the career ladder is to stop doing the job she's trained for.'

Helen nodded. 'I suppose so. Well, I know so really, but I think it's wrong. That's not what most of us go into nursing for, is it? I know I wouldn't want to move into management. I enjoy the practical side of things too much. But that's easy to say when, hopefully, I won't have to rely on my own income for much longer. If you have to support yourself it can't be as easy.'

'You mean—' Abbey struggled to maintain her composure despite feeling as if Helen's words had actually punched her in the ribs '—you mean you're getting married?'

Helen smiled shyly. 'I shouldn't have said anything, really, but I long to be able to chat about him freely. He's a local GP, you see, and we have to be careful until his divorce comes through.'

Although she hadn't been conscious of holding her breath, the relief Abbey felt at the news caused it to rush from her body in a deep sigh. 'In that case my lips are sealed, but you are more than welcome to talk things over with me any time.'

'Thanks. I'll remember that. Hopefully it shouldn't be too long now.' As Helen closed the door behind her Abbey leaned back in her chair and pondered the unexpected news. What a stupid fool she'd been. Determined not to become the object of a hospital rumour herself, she'd been only too ready to believe the gossip where Max and Helen were concerned—making it impossible for her to accept that Max could have any kind of a commitment towards her.

She'd been too busy protecting herself from future hurt to believe that his feelings for her might just be genuine.

No wonder he was exasperated by her rejections. When she thought of all the ways he'd tried to prove he really did care only to have her accuse him of doing it to get his own way, her heart sank.

One thing was now clear. If she wasn't to spend the rest of her life living with her regrets, she must let Max know how she truly felt.

And sooner rather than later. Hopefully it wasn't too late to give their relationship another chance, and if it didn't work out as she hoped at least she would have tried.

Having come to that decision, Abbey become increasingly disappointed as the week passed with the only word from him a message to say that the nurse with the bad back was fine and at work again.

It was as if he'd taken enough rebuffs and was not

going to risk more. During her ward rounds Denny
talked about him incessantly, so it was almost a relief
when he was discharged.

'I hope he does what he's told this time,' she said
to Penny.

Penny smiled. 'I think he's learned his lesson.'

Max's absence at least gave her a chance to get on
with her work uninterrupted, but as the number of
days without a sight of him lengthened beyond the
week her anxiety grew. And yet she couldn't blame
him. Wouldn't she have felt the same if she had
received even half the rebuffs she'd handed out?

'I must pop out to the bank,' she told Jane early
on Thursday morning after another night of disturbed
sleep. 'I need more information before I can finalise
these figures for the auditors this afternoon. Town
should be reasonably quiet at the moment, so it should
only take about half an hour.'

'No problem,' Jane told her. 'I'll hold the fort—I
don't mind now Mr Darby has become less persistent!
He was a bit frightening at first.'

Abbey laughed to hide her disquiet at his prolonged
absence from her office. 'I told you he's never been
known to be physically violent.'

'I'll believe you.' Jane returned her attention to her
keyboard.

Finding the main street almost deserted, Abbey was
able to park outside the bank and quickly carry out
her transactions. She was about to unlock her car and
return to the hospital when, out of the corner of her
eye, she saw a man collapse onto the pavement outside
the post office.

She rushed across the road to see if she could help
and to her horror discovered that she recognised the
man. It was Mr Murray, who had had a hip replacement such a short time ago.

Offering a silent prayer for her ex-patient, her

immediate concern was to prevent anyone moving him
into a position that might undo the success of his operation. She crouched down beside him. 'Hello, Mr
Murray. Remember me? I'm the manager from
St Luke's. Have you hurt yourself?'

The old man shook his head, tears in his rheumy
eyes. 'I'm not sure. Just leave me to collect myself a
minute.' He moved each leg experimentally in turn,
and she was pleased to see that there didn't seem to
be any problem.

'It was me pension he was after, you know.'

Abbey was horrified. 'You mean—you mean someone knocked you down?' Despite the earlier empty
street, a crowd had gathered by this time, but Abbey
had been too concerned about Mr Murray to notice
anyone running away.

The elderly man shrugged. 'He kicked my stick
away. But he didn't get any money. I saw to that.'

'Have you any pain?' she asked him again.

He shook his head. 'No. I don't seem to have hurt
myself anywhere. But what about my hip? Will it be
all right, miss?'

'I'll get someone to help me move you gradually to
your feet and then decide what to do. If all seems well,
I'll run you home and then get someone to take a look
at you there. Otherwise I'll call an ambulance. OK?'

When he nodded she started to help him up. 'If you
feel any discomfort anywhere, give a shout and I'll
stop immediately.'

Abbey gradually helped him to a comfortable position and from there to his feet. Disappointed that
it was nothing more exciting, the crowd was rapidly
melting away, but a gum-chewing youth, wearing
scruffy jeans and a demin jacket, remained behind
to help.

Thinking that you could never judge by appearances,
Abbey smiled up at him. 'If you could just walk with

us as far as my car over there,' she said to the lad. 'Just in case.'

Once Mr Murray was safely in the car, Abbey thanked the youth and he sauntered away down the street.

Mr Murray muttered. 'Cocky beggar. He did it, you know.'

'Did what?'

'That lad who helped. He was the one who kicked the stick away.'

'Surely not!' Abbey exclaimed. Convinced that Mr Murray must be mistaken, she added, 'He'd never have stayed to help if he had been. They all tend to look alike in their denims, you know. It's a kind of uniform.'

He shook his head. 'I'm not wrong. He was hoping you'd leave me in his care. Then he could have finished the job.'

'Why on earth didn't you say so at the time? Someone in the crowd would have called the police.'

He shrugged. 'What for? They'd let him off. Say he had an unhappy childhood or something.'

Abbey didn't argue. She felt it more important to get him safely home and checked over. 'Where do you live?'

'Downs Road. Other side of the dual carriageway. You need to go up to the double roundabout.'

'Is there anyone at home?'

'No. I live alone. I have help a couple of times a week, but not today.'

Abbey set off the way he'd suggested and, with his directions, soon found the house.

'Now, before I help you out, where's your doorkey?'

He handed it to Abbey and, after carefully helping him onto his feet, she locked the car before assisting him slowly into the house.

'Is there anyone I can contact to be with you for the rest of the day?'

'No. I'll be all right.'

Despite his claim, she could see that he was plainly shaken by the events of the morning, and so didn't give much credence to his earlier accusation. OK, the boy *had* looked rough, but she couldn't believe he would have had the gall to offer his help in the hope that he'd have another opportunity to get his hands on Mr Murray's money.

However, once she could safely leave her ex-patient she would return to the post office and see if anyone there had seen anything to support Mr Murray's story, and if so, she would have no problem in describing the assailant to the police.

She helped Mr Murray in to a high armchair and, after lighting the gas fire nearby, asked, 'Would you like a cup of something?'

'Tea, please.'

Abbey made her way into the kitchen and filled the kettle. While she waited for it to boil, she washed some of the dirty crockery on the side. 'Sugar and milk?' she called.

Receiving no answer, she returned to the living room and found Mr Murray asleep.

Best thing for him, she told herself, but where does that leave me? I told Jane I wouldn't be long. She quickly checked around but found no sign of a telephone and didn't feel she could risk going out in search of one.

All she could do was drink the cup of tea she'd made and wait.

It was over an hour later that he stirred and eventually woke up properly. 'I think the tea's probably cold now,' Abbey joked. 'I'll make another pot.'

'I feel better for the nap.' He looked it, too.

'You're not on the telephone, are you, Mr Murray?' she asked when she'd settled him with his drink.

He chuckled. 'I've a mobile in my pocket. Who do you want to ring?'

'I think your GP ought to check you over and I must let my secretary know where I am.'

'I'm fine. I don't need the GP; he's more than useless. Too long in the tooth.' Abbey hid her amusement as he went on to say, 'But you can ring the hospital if you like.' He slowly pulled the telephone from his pocket and, opening it, handed it to Abbey.

She dialled the hospital number and asked to be put through to Jane.

'Where on earth have you been?' her secretary asked on hearing her voice. 'I rang the bank and—'

'One of our ex-patients had a fall—I took him home.'

'Where are you?'

'Downs Road.'

She could hear Jane relaying her answers and asked who was with her.

'Mr Darby. I knew you intended to come straight back to work on the report for the auditors so I wondered where you could have got to. I was checking if your car was in the car park when I met Mr Darby.'

'Abbey—' Max had obviously taken the receiver from Jane '—are you all right?'

'Of course. Why shouldn't I be?' she responded, although pleased that he cared sufficiently to ask. 'It was your hip replacement, Mr Murray, who fell, and I thought I ought to see him safely home.'

'Has he done any damage?'

'I don't think so.'

'Have you had him checked over?'

'He doesn't want me to call his GP.'

'Stay where you are,' Max barked. 'I'm coming right over. What number Downs Road?'

Abbey told him and, closing the telephone, she handed it back to Mr Murray. 'You're going to have

that hip checked whether you like it or not,' she told
him with a smile of relief. 'Mr Darby was in my secretary's office and wants to see for himself that you
haven't undone his handiwork. He'll be here
before long.'

'I'd rather have him than my GP!' he told her with
a twinkle in his eye. 'And I bet you would too.'

'I don't know what you mean,' she protested.

'Mr Darby's much better looking!'

Abbey responded, 'You're a rogue, but I must say
I'm pleased Mr Darby is going to look you over. If he
says you're OK, I can leave you without worrying.'

It wasn't long before she heard a car draw up and,
peering through the window, saw that it was Max arriving. She opened the front door.

He marched straight through to Mr Murray. 'What
have you been doing?'

'It wasn't my fault,' he protested. 'One of they young
thugs kicked my stick away. Wanted my pension,
he did.'

Abbey looked at Max and shrugged. 'I noticed him
falling, but didn't see how it happened. He thinks the
lad who helped me to right him was the culprit.'

'And what do you think?'

'I find it difficult to believe.'

'Have you contacted the police?'

Abbey shook her head. 'I've only just discovered
that Mr Murray has a mobile phone in his pocket.'

'Can you describe the youth?'

Abbey nodded. 'Yes, but my main concern was to
get Mr Murray home.'

Max nodded approvingly and turned his attention to
his patient. 'Let's have a look at you, then.'

After a very thorough examination, Max patted Mr
Murray on the shoulder. 'I don't think you've done
any damage.'

'I didn't think I had.'

'What are you going to do about lunch?' Abbey was
keen to get back to work, but didn't want to leave Mr
Murray unless he had everything he needed.

'The meals on wheels will be here before long. And
you don't need to wait. They have a key.'

She lifted his cup and saucer. 'Another drink?'

Mr Murray shook his head. 'No. I'm fine. Get along
with you both.'

As they closed the front door behind them,
Max smiled warmly and said, 'Thanks for taking
such good care of him. You probably stopped shock
setting in.'

Warmed by his praise, Abbey said, 'I'm only glad I
was on the spot.'

'I don't think it's a good idea to inform the police
about the supposed assault. As you say, he was probably mistaken and I think it's more important for him
to be left to rest quietly.'

Abbey frowned. 'Perhaps you're right. I would hate
a good Samaritan to be mistakenly accused. It'd probably be the last time he helped anyone.'

As they unlocked their separate cars, Abbey told
him, 'I'll call at the post office on the way through
and check if anyone there saw anything untoward. If
they did, I'll go on to the police station and suggest
they keep the post office area under observation when
pensions are being paid.'

None of the three post-office staff had seen anything.
'Have you noticed any youths hanging around
recently?' Abbey asked them.

Again the reply was negative. Sure now that Mr
Murray must have been mistaken, she thanked them
for their help and returned to the hospital to get on
with her delayed financial report.

She was surprised to find Max waiting in Jane's
empty office when she arrived back at the hospital.

'How did it go?' he greeted her.

'No one saw anything.' She nodded towards the empty desk. 'Where's Jane?'

'She's slipped out for a short lunch break. How about us doing the same?'

Abbey closed her eyes and sighed with frustration. Having made up her mind to jump at every opportunity Max offered, she was genuinely sorry that she couldn't accept.

Especially as she was now determined to try and resolve the misunderstandings between them. But she knew it wasn't going to be easy. And that it was something that could not be rushed.

'I'm sorry, Max, I'd love to but I've the auditors coming at half past one and a morning's worth of work to prepare for them!' Cursing her bad luck, she checked her watch again but knew it was impossible. She'd been absolutely determined not to refuse another of his invitations if one should be forthcoming, but this was urgent.

'There's nothing I'd like better, Max. But I can't today. I only popped out to the bank for a few minutes. I needed some figures to finalise my report and I'd left just enough time to work it all out. Time that I then lost with Mr Murray.'

She wached his expression change to one of defeat with a plummeting heart. 'Please, Max. It's the truth. I know I've made excuses in the past, but this time I would come if I possibly could.'

It was obvious that he didn't believe her. 'Remember what I said about all work and no play?'

'I do remember, Max, and if I hadn't this meeting I'd honestly jump at the chance.' She sought desperately for a way to convince him. 'Any other day this week there would be no problem, but if I'm not prepared for this afternoon's meeting I'll have Mr Barratt down on me like a ton of bricks.'

He shrugged and, recognising that she was in an

impossible position, she attempted to salvage the situation by offering, 'I could get a meal for us this evening?'

'That's mighty generous of you,' he responded derisively, 'but I'm afraid I'm otherwise engaged then.'

It was Abbey's turn not to believe him, but she could do nothing except watch him swing round on his heel and stride from the office.

And, what was worse, she couldn't blame him. She brushed away a tear as she thought of all the opportunities she had so heedlessly thrown away, and wished with all her heart that she'd behaved differently.

However, her paperwork had to be done, so, attempting to push her regrets to the back of her mind, she poured herself a cup of coffee and tried to concentrate on her work.

Over the next few days Max was again conspicuous by his absence, but Abbey tried to convince herself that it was due to the increased number of operations he was now able to carry out. In contrast with her private life, she seemed to be making a success of her job as a manager. Her business plan was working well and the number of admissions was growing daily.

For the first time since she had started at St Luke's she looked forward to the MedCom meeting the following Wednesday, not only because she was able to report that the number of forward bookings for surgery was the highest since the hospital opened, but because she knew it would be a chance to see Max again.

However, after his opening remarks, when he studiously avoided meeting her eyes, she wished she'd had a chance to talk to him before the meeting.

Trying to ignore her personal feelings, Abbey announced the upturn in business proudly. 'We have also granted admitting rights to more surgeons. If we go on at this rate we'll soon need to expand the facilities.' She made the joke partly to reassure those present that they wouldn't lose the more flexible working arrangements they were now enjoying, and partly because she was finding it increasingly difficult to talk with Max's hostile gaze upon her.

When, after much discussion, the refreshments arrived, he came over and, with an ironic lift of an eyebrow, shook her hand and said, 'Fantastic news, Abbey. You must be really pleased with your success. I was wrong, after all. You *are* in the right job.'

The tender shoots of her emotions, rawly exposed by his touch, were deeply wounded by his damning praise.

Swallowing hard, she forced herself to return his smile and speak calmly. 'Just taking on that extra theatre nurse made a tremendous difference. It's allowed me to increase the the number of permanent ward staff, which in turn makes the hospital able to handle even more cases.'

'I can't resist saying I told you so. I did warn you I would gloat if the business suffered because you wouldn't do what I suggested. So I think I'm entitled to gloat when you did, and it's successful.'

'Don't think you deserve all the credit.' Having decided that they were going to get nowhere fast if their conversation remained so formal, she accompanied the reproach with a teasing smile. 'I would have taken the same action if only you'd given me a chance to find out the true position before barging in with your suggestions.' She smiled again, hoping to lighten the tension between them, but not a muscle on his face as much as twitched. 'Once I was allowed to work things out with my staff, I could see the need myself.'

'I'm sure you could and for all our sakes I'm glad it's worked out. You must certainly think your change of occupation worthwhile.'

Humiliated by his pompous tone, she wanted to say more—much more—but while he remained so unbending she knew it was hopeless.

However, she would never forgive herself if she didn't try. 'Max,' she eventually said breathlessly, conscious of the hammering of her heart against her ribs, 'I know this is the wrong time and place, but—'

'It always is,' he interrupted. 'Sorry, Abbey, I must catch Ellie.'

Unable to believe his indifference, she knew that at that moment she would have willingly exchanged her success as a manager for a return to the rapport they had once shared.

How could the situation have changed in such a short time? He was now saying that he thought she was in the right job, while she was rapidly coming to the conclusion that he'd been right from the beginning. She *had* enjoyed assisting him in Theatre again and, despite the outcome, taking care of Mrs Jenkins had given her as much if not greater satisfaction. Making a financial success of the business certainly wasn't giving her anywhere near the same sense of achievement.

'Let's go,' she heard Max say to Ellie as the room rapidly emptied. They left together, and if Abbey hadn't already been convinced of the fact their togetherness would have made it clear that she had left it far too late. It wasn't work that was keeping him away from her. He'd given up the chase and obviously there were plenty of others only too ready to leap at his invitations.

CHAPTER TEN

ABBEY left the hospital that evening thankful that she didn't have to return to an empty flat. Ben was still in hospital. The new treatment regime didn't seem to be having the desired effect and Abbey couldn't help wondering if he was receiving the placebo treatment.

Cheryl's employers allowed her time off to visit him in the afternoons. However, she found that the evenings dragged without Ben around. So she had invited Abbey for supper as soon as the MedCom meeting finished.

As she drove away from the hospital Abbey looked forward to their get-together as a means of obliterating Max's comments from her mind.

Cheryl was a creative cook who enjoyed sharing her meals, and Abbey felt so despondent that evening that she knew she wouldn't have bothered to cook for herself.

'Well? How did the meeting go?' Cheryl asked as she followed Abbey into the sitting room.

'OK.'

'Only OK? I thought you were going to wow them with your news—or has the business suffered a sudden setback?'

'No. I think they were all delighted.'

Cheryl frowned. 'Come on, Abbey, what's the problem? I was expecting you to be over the moon. Instead you look as if you've just won the pools and not posted your coupon!'

Abbey laughed. 'Sorry, Cheryl. I seem to have a lot on my mind besides work. But I did say I was coming to cheer you up, so I'll snap out of it. How is Ben?'

'Better this afternoon. Perhaps they'll let him home before long. Now, I want to know what you can possibly have on your mind. You've a good job, a nice home and. . .' she hesitated and nodded. 'That's your problem, isn't it? No one to share it with.'

Abbey started to protest but Cheryl ignored her. 'Right, it's my turn to do something for you.'

Recognising that her friend was up to something, Abbey grinned defensively. 'Honestly, I'm fine.'

'Maybe, but you'll be even better with a man around the house. Now I've had a good idea.'

'I guessed as much!'

'The rugby lads have arranged a post-practice supper tomorrow evening. Very informal. There are quite a few new players and it's so they can all get to know one another and any partners. Surprisingly, the new ones are nearly all eligible bachelors. Come and meet them. Mr Right might just be amongst them!'

'I doubt it.' Abbey now knew only too well who Mr Right was, but she'd thrown away any chance of convincing him of the fact.

'Don't be so defeatist, Abbey. I keep telling you, you need to get out more. This is your opportunity. You will come, won't you? Not only for your sake. I'd appreciate the company.'

'OK, in that case I'll come, but you're not to try any matchmaking.'

'I wouldn't dream of it.' Cheryl grinned wickedly.

Thursday dragged for Abbey. Max's behaviour the evening before had robbed her work of its attraction. She would even have been glad of a problem rearing its ugly head, but there was nothing. Just routine paperwork. Late in the afternoon she decided to do a ward round and chat to some of the patients. It was the first task she had enjoyed all day.

She joined Penny in the ward office for a cup of tea.

'Mr Tate looks well now, doesn't he?'

'He's going home tomorrow. He could have gone before but organising some of the community services he needed wasn't easy.' Penny smiled. 'Mr Renny keeps telling us what a good job we're doing with him. It's nice to have a consultant so appreciative for once, rather than complaining.'

'Talking of complaining,' Abbey joked, 'is there a reason why Mr Darby doesn't have any in-patients at the moment?'

Although she made the query as casually as she could, she held her breath until Penny reassured her that he hadn't taken his business elsewhere. Flicking through her diary, she told Abbey, 'He has a couple booked in for next week.'

'That's OK, then.' Abbey was relieved that at least their enmity wasn't affecting the business. 'Keep up the good work.'

As she left the hospital that evening she bumped into Tom Renny.

'I hear Mr Tate is going home. We'll miss our star patient.'

'I'm delighted with how well he's done. Considering what happened, your staff have worked marvels with him in a relatively short time. I'll buy you a drink at our little celebration this evening. After all, we owe the hospital's improved success to you.'

Abbey frowned. 'Er—I can't—I didn't know—'

Mr Renny seemed surprised. 'As it seems we have something to celebrate, Max suggested yesterday that we all go out for a curry tonight. Surely he didn't omit to tell you?'

'Er, no—well, I'd probably already said I was going out.' Abbey knew she was blustering and didn't expect him to believe her, but she just had to get away.

'That's a pity. Next time, perhaps.' He scrutinised her closely as he held the main door open for her, and she sped across the car park, her cheeks flaming.

Throughout the long day, Abbey had quite looked forward to the evening out. It would be something different and Cheryl was always good company. Now she couldn't imagine feeling less like going. But she couldn't let her friend down and not turn up.

Cheryl had obviously given up any hope of Abbey joining them by the time she had sufficiently recovered her composure to change into a sweater and jeans and drive to the rugby club.

'Wanted to make an entrance, did you?' she teased as Abbey self-consciously made her way across the crowded room, removing her suede jacket as she walked.

'Not exactly,' Abbey replied. 'It wasn't the best of nights to choose. I—er—wanted to do a ward round. One of our long-stay patients is going home tomorrow and in case he leaves early I wanted to wish him well.'

'Ben's dad apologises for not being here. One of the team has done something painful to his knee so they've gone to sort it out. Grab a drink and I'll do the honours.'

'The honours?' Abbey queried suspiciously.

'Introduce you to a few people.'

'A few men, you mean.' Abbey grinned wryly.

Cheryl was unabashed. 'That's why I invited you!'

As Cheryl kept to her word, Abbey was suddenly conscious of her age. Every one of the unattached men being promoted appeared to be at least ten years younger, and so immature. She couldn't help comparing them with Max, and every one of them came a very definite second.

'I've kept the best till last,' Cheryl whispered in her ear as she dragged Abbey across the room. 'This is Kevin, Dad's new recruit.'

Thankful that he was the last of Cheryl's hopefuls,

Abbey craned her neck upwards to meet the interested gaze of a stockily built male.

'Abbey is the manager of St Luke's Hospital,' Cheryl told him proudly.

His expression changed to one of distaste. 'One of the many, no doubt!'

'What do you mean?' Abbey enquired defensively.

'The whole health service is sinking under the weight of administrators,' he told her bitterly.

'St Luke's is a private hospital,' Cheryl rushed to inform him.

'So? Does that make it any better? It's still the nurses who do the work and the managers who get the money.'

'I am a trained nurse,' Abbey told him coolly, 'and have moved into management to try and improve the lot of nurses.'

He didn't appear in the least affected by her put-down, but shrugged and muttered darkly, 'I shouldn't think you'll succeed for one moment.'

'You seem knowledgeable. Do you work in a hospital?'

He laughed. 'Not exactly. Hey, I'm starving. Why don't we all wander over to the buffet?'

Cheryl said hurriedly, 'Kevin's a medical student.'

He was already halfway across the room so Abbey whispered, 'I'm not so desperate that I need to cradle-snatch. I stopped going out with medical students when I finished my training!'

Cheryl grinned. 'He's not as young as you think. He's already a dentist but he wants to be a consultant so he's doing a second degree.'

They'd caught up with Kevin by that time, so Abbey said quietly, 'I see.'

'These vol-au-vents are tasty.' He offered the plate to the two girls, but Abbey refused.

'No, thanks. I'm not really hungry.'

The three of them made desultory conversation while Kevin ate and, though Abbey found him pleasant enough to talk to for an evening, that was all. So when they were separated by a sudden rush for food she was unconcerned and wandered off to chat with some of the others she'd been introduced to.

When later she asked if she could phone for a taxi, Cheryl tried to pair them up again. 'There's no need. Kevin will drop you home. I've already asked him.'

'But—'

'He's only been drinking tonic water. I promise.'

Abbey could do nothing but accept the lift. 'I'm sorry to drag you away from the party,' she told him when Cheryl beckoned him over.

'No problem. I've an essay to write before I go to bed.'

As they left, Cheryl beamed after them like a satisfied mother hen and Abbey could have cheerfully murdered her.

'Why don't you like nursing?' As they approached the main road Kevin was watching her reaction to his provocative question rather than where he was going.

He pulled straight out into the path of another car. There wasn't time for either driver to take avoiding action and as she waited for the inevitable jolt Abbey closed her eyes.

When she opened them she saw, with horror, Max climbing from the hired Astra, before stooping to examine the damage to the nearside wing.

She groaned and closed her eyes again, hoping the nightmare would go away. They'd been on an emotional collision course since her first day in the job and now this! In a car with a lunatic driver she hardly knew!

'Are you OK?' Her groan had obviously worried Kevin.

'Yes—just unwilling to meet the driver of that car. I seem to put a jinx on whatever he drives.' She lowered her head to hide tears of frustration at nothing ever going right.

'Blimey, he looks determined. You say you know him?'

She hurriedly wiped her eyes and turned to see Max striding purposefully towards them.

As Kevin wound down the window, a furious Max poked his head inside and, about to bawl at Kevin, recoiled at the sight of Abbey in the passenger seat.

'I don't believe it!' He turned to Kevin. 'What the hell do you think you were playing at?'

'I—I— My attention was distracted.'

Max glared at Abbey. 'I can well imagine.' Ignoring the pleading look in her eyes, he almost imperceptibly shook his head. 'I should hate to intrude on your cosy tête-à-tête, so I'll expect you to let me have all his insurance details tomorrow.' He strode angrily back to his own car and, after another look at the damage, drove away at speed.

'Phew! When I saw the size of him I thought I was in for it. Thank goodness he knew you. Do you work with him?'

'In a way. Look, I can walk from here. There's a short cut. I'm very grateful for the lift but I could do with some air. Goodnight, Kevin.'

'If you're sure—but I'd better give you some details for your colleague first.' He took out a card and scribbled for a few moments. 'Tell him to ring me if he wants any other info.'

'Thanks. And for the lift.' When he didn't raise any objection to her leaving, but instead seemed as relieved as she was, she let out the breath she'd been unconsciously holding. She just wanted to escape and forget that any of this had happened.

As she rounded the corner from the Spread Eagle, she saw Max's car parked outside her flat. When he looked up and saw her he threw open the driver's door and strode towards her, his anger evident. 'That idiot hasn't let you walk home unaccompanied? What an absolute. . . I—I don't believe. . . Words honestly fail me.'

Abbey muttered, 'I don't see what it has to do with you, or why you are spying on me here.'

He shook his head sadly. 'I don't expect you do, but when I'd calmed down a bit I realised I should have checked you were OK after that crunch so I thought it best to wait here for you to arrive. Does he always drive that way?'

Wondering if he'd also intended to have another go at Kevin, she shrugged. 'I've no idea, I—' A warmth was stirring deep within her at him caring enough to bother, and she wanted to explain why she'd been in Kevin's car, but he interrupted.

'I should have thought him barely old enough to have passed his test. I can't see what you see in such a—a. . .'

'For goodness' sake, Max, I don't see anything in him—my friend asked him to drive me home, that's all. If you're fishing to find out if that's Ben, I can tell you now it's not.'

'I know.'

She swung her head round sharply. 'How do you know?'

'I should have thought that was obvious. If you'd shacked up with him ten years ago you'd have been sleeping with a preteen. So who is he?'

'I don't think that's any of your business.'

'I think it is, Abbey,' he told her, the anger in his voice replaced by a softer tone. 'You see, I was actually on my way to see you when that idiot ran into me.'

'To see *me*?' Abbey was instantly on the alert. 'Is something wrong at the hospital?'

'Calm down. It's nothing to do with work. I just wanted to talk to you.'

'Can't it wait?'

'Before I tell you why I chose this moment, I need to know what that chap means to you.'

'I told you—nothing,' she retorted. 'And I have no intention of discussing it out here. So you'd better either leave it until tomorrow or come in.'

Her temper flaring at his unreasonable demand, she strode up the garden path and let herself in through the front door without a backward glance. However, she was acutely aware that he was following her. What on earth did he want to say that was suddenly so urgent?

'Coffee?' she asked as she closed the door behind him.

'That would be nice.'

Uncomfortably conscious of him hovering beside her, she led the way into the sitting room and switched on the room heater. 'Make yourself comfortable. I won't be a moment.' Despite a struggle to control it, her voice wavered.

She started to move towards the kitchen, but her progress was halted by Max grasping her shoulder and turning her gently to face him.

She reluctantly raised her eyes to meet his gaze, and was surprised to read an unexpected concern there. 'Sit down and I'll do the coffee. That chap deserves a good kicking for allowing you to walk home after giving you such a scare.'

Unwilling to let him know that it wasn't the accident but his presence that was affecting her, she murmured, 'It wasn't his fault. I insisted.' She hesitated, then reached into the pocket of her suede jacket. 'Here's his business card, by the way, with insurance details on the back.' While she spoke she allowed herself to be lowered onto the settee.

He pushed the card into his trouser pocket. 'You've

had quite an evening of it, one way or another, haven't you? Coffee'll revive us both.'

'I'm sorry, Max. I'm not thinking straight. The accident must have shaken you as well.'

He grinned. 'It was all over before I realised what was happening. You probably saw it coming and that's much worse.'

'What do you want to talk about?'

'All in good time. Coffee first.'

He moved into the kitchen and Abbey could hear him opening cupboards until he found what he required.

Having made two mugs of coffee, he brought them through and, handing her one, sat down beside her.

'Now, tell me about him.'

She put her mug down on the coffee-table. 'The car driver you mean?' To give herself time, she removed her jacket and threw it over the arm of a chair. 'He's a dentist.'

'A dentist!' echoed Max incredulously. 'He ought to know better, then.' He took the business card from his pocket and slowly shook his head. 'He looks, and behaves, more like a student.'

'He is a student. He's doing a medical degree now.'

'Ah! A high-flyer. Now I understand.'

'Understand what?' Abbey demanded sharply.

'You said yourself you wanted to get to the top—what better way to do it than to marry a high-flyer?'

'Max!' Abbey didn't try to hide her exasperation. 'How many times do I have to tell you that he means absolutely nothing to me? I only met him this evening when a friend asked him to drive me home.'

'That'd be Cheryl, would it?'

About to take a sip of her coffee, Abbey lowered the mug to the table again and asked suspiciously, 'What do you know about Cheryl?'

Max didn't speak but inclined his head knowingly.

'Cheryl and I have been friends since we were at school.'

'And her husband, Ben?'

Abbey didn't know where he'd got the information, but it began to explain why he was behaving so oddly.

'Is this why you were so angry out there?'

'I *was* angry—bloody angry—at that—that idiot first of all putting your life at risk by driving like a maniac and then letting you walk the rest of the way home in the dark. If I could have laid my hands on him at the moment I saw you come round the corner alone, I wouldn't have been responsible for my actions.'

'It really was my fault, Max. I insisted. I know the short cuts.'

'If you think that excuses him, it doesn't. In fact, it makes matters worse. He should know better than to allow you to come through dark alleyways at this time of night. It shows a distinct lack of responsibility. Especially when you might be suffering from shock. I can't believe he didn't insist on seeing you home. Anything could have happened.'

Recalling his own insistence on seeing her home on the night of Melissa's dinner party, she felt a glow spread through her that had nothing to do with the coffee. 'Nice to know you care,' she told him flippantly to hide her embarrassment.

'I hope you know by now that I *do* care—I've tried to tell you often enough.'

'That's where you're wrong, Max,' she told him quietly. 'I don't know. That's why I've tried to keep you at arm's length.'

He watched her expectantly. 'You blame me for our break-up all those years ago, don't you? I can assure you I did not break my word—'

'Oh, yes, you—'

'Hear me out, Abbey,' Max insisted quietly. 'I was

called out to see a rugby player this evening who'd injured his knee at practice.'

Unable to see what that had to do with his feelings for her, Abbey waited suspiciously.

'The club chairman brought him to St Luke's. A chap called Jack Wickham.' Abbey saw a teasing glint in his eyes. 'I believe you know him?'

She nodded slowly, recognising only too well where Max had learnt about Cheryl and Ben. But the fact that he now knew the truth still didn't excuse his past behaviour.

'While I waited for X-rays to be done, Jack Wickham and I had a very interesting chat. He said a lot of nice things about St Luke's new manager. In fact, he said what a wonderful person she is.'

Abbey felt the colour flaring in her cheeks.

'I asked him if he'd known you long, and he replied, "Know her? She's been like a daughter to me. Especially since her own father died. She was devoted to him." Of course *I* knew that, but I asked how he knew. He told me his son went to school with you. As did his son's wife. And that you are all still close friends.

'I was about to change the subject when Jack said, "Abbey was marvellous when Cheryl was studying for her law degree. I could never have coped with Ben on my own at the time."'

Knowing what must come next, Abbey couldn't meet his searching gaze and closed her eyes.

'I asked why he couldn't cope and he told me that his son, who has multiple sclerosis, had a bad patch just as Cheryl was doing her finals. He told me you moved in to help.' Watching her reaction, he took her hand between his. 'I'm sure you understand. At that moment I felt as if I'd been hit with a sledgehammer.'

Abbey rushed in to try and explain. 'Ben likes to be treated as a normal adult, and Cheryl knew I understood. When he's in a good phase, he lives and works like everybody else. Unfortunately the bad times are coming more often now, and he has to use a wheelchair.'

'A wheelchair,' Max echoed faintly. 'And yet his father does so much for the rugby club.' He shook his head in disbelief.

'He does it for Ben's sake. As he can't take part, he likes to be involved behind the scenes and it's surprising what he can manage to do.'

'Why on earth didn't you tell me all this before?' He released her hand and turned her so that he could see her face.

Ashamed of the way she had deceived him, Abbey didn't answer. And she was still unclear as to how any of this made any difference to her believing what he had to say.

'I asked Jack when it was that you moved in to help. When he told me, everything fell into place.'

Abbey thought back. 'It was about ten years ago. Just after you left—'

'I know. Jack said.' He lowered his head into his hands. 'Oh, Abbey, what a fool I've been. I've wasted all these years believing you'd been two-timing me and not realising that all the time you thought I'd broken my word. But when we met up again, why didn't you ask instead of letting me think you were still in the midst of an affair?'

Abbey dropped her gaze and murmured, 'I didn't want to be humiliated further. So. . .' she searched for the right words '. . .I—I thought it best to pretend I hadn't cared about you.'

'And all the time you did?'

She looked up to meet his gaze and nodded. 'I suppose I did.' She laughed wryly. 'But all this still doesn't explain—'

'I know,' he told her gently. 'I realise now I should have said something long ago. But I didn't think you were interested. That's why I rushed round here the moment I'd heard what Jack had to say about you taking care of Ben.'

Abbey frowned. 'That's all very well, Max, but I didn't move in until a good month after you'd gone off to do your locum jobs and you didn't ring me once in that time.'

'The first job I took was a flight to northern India to bring back an injured ex-pat. When I landed there was trouble with the Sikhs. They were torching the temples and rioting at the airport, preventing any planes from taking off. All the lines were down and I couldn't get in touch with you, or anyone else. The moment I got back to this country I tried, and failed.

'When your ex-flatmate told me you had moved in with a chap whose father could help your career I was furious. I wanted to find you and confront you but when I calmed down I decided that if you were happy it was best to forget you and leave things as they were. But, as I said before, it wasn't that easy. Incidentally, why did your flatmate think Jack could help your career?'

Abbey laughed. 'He *was* chairman of the regional health authority but, funnily enough, resigned to help with Ben at the same time as I moved in. I'd no idea that was what she thought.'

'Just goes to show how easy it is to get the wrong idea. When you were appointed to St Luke's and I discovered you weren't married I was sure we were being given a second chance. I couldn't wait to meet up with you, but you definitely thought differently.'

'Oh, Max! Ten wasted years.'

'Not totally wasted,' he reassured her tenderly. 'We've both progressed in our careers and in our own ways tried to use our skills to help those less fortunate. You see, it was while I was stranded out in India that I learnt about this hospital train that I support.' He took her in his arms and, with a confident smile in his eyes, captured her face between his powerful hands and found her mouth with the warm, firm lips she remembered so well.

Helplessly she abandoned all thought of distrust and submitted to the invasion of her senses. Her body was crying out for him as it had that night at the hotel, but this time she saw no reason not to take what she wanted so badly.

Contrite now, she wanted to explain, and murmured, 'When you came back into my life, first of all I expected you to be married, and by the time I discovered you weren't I was in no doubt that Helen was destined for that role.'

'Helen?'

'What else could I think? I saw you leaving the hospital together and when I needed you to look at Andy she was obviously embarrassed when I recognised her voice. That was why I was so furious when you started to come on so strongly. I thought you were only trying to cajole me into agreeing to your demands for the hospital. And after our visit to the Mercy I decided you just wanted to resume our earlier affair and I couldn't bear to be hurt again. That's why I kept up the pretence about Ben.'

Conscious of his laughter, she asked, 'What's the joke?'

'I think I've only taken Helen home once and that was because her car had failed its MOT. I have to confess we conspired to pressurise you in the beginning, but we soon realised nothing was going to make you change your mind.

'And the night you needed my services at St Luke's—' he could hardly talk for laughing '—Helen was doing bank work at another hospital. I'd asked her to help and she didn't want you to know.'

'What she does in her spare time is her business!'

'I told her that, but she was afraid you'd be furious when St Luke's was so short of theatre staff.'

He nodded sagely. 'Now I understand why you played so hard to get when your body was telling me such a different story.'

He swept her up into his arms again and his lips met hers with a gentle apology before he murmured, 'I wouldn't have hurt you for the world all those years ago.' He grinned widely. 'Apart from the day I thought you'd been two-timing me, that is!'

He pressed his lips back firmly onto hers, this time possessively exploring their contours, his moist tongue searching for an entry point.

Abbey's uncontrollable response raised an awareness of just what she had missed and she clung to him, her senses clamouring for much more while her mind struggled to free itself from the restraints with which she had protected herself for so long.

The sense of loss as they eventually moved apart made her want to cling onto him, to be sure that this time nothing would part them. He must have recognised her need for, sliding his arms round her shoulders, he pulled her close and whispered into her hair, 'Oh, Abbey, love, you're not going to get away this time. I love you far too much to waste one more minute away from you.'

She breathed in steadily and, with tears of happiness trickling down her cheek, she found the courage to tell him what she had wanted to tell him for so long. 'I love you, Max. I always have and always will.'

He sighed deeply. 'I've hoped to hear that for so long. My darling, darling girl.'

As his arms went around her, strong and supportive, she raised her head to meet his lips halfway. Lost in the tenderness of his touch, she felt herself being eased beneath his body, and, instinctively recognising that it was where she belonged, all her fears dissolved.

This time she could indulge the ache within.

His fingers caressingly traced the length of her collar-bone and slid across her shoulders before moving gently down to trace the curve of her breasts beneath her sweater. 'I still can't quite believe this. I thought you'd grown into such a hard person that day you took up your post here. I found it difficult to believe you were the same Abbey I'd known all those years ago. But you are.' With his free hand he cupped the eager peak straining towards him and dropped a light kiss on her lips. 'In fact, I'm beginning to discover you're just a softie under that hard exterior.'

As her body responded to his every movement, she couldn't help giggling.

Pretending to be hurt, Max said, 'Hey! I was being serious.'

'I know, but I can't help thinking you're trying to tell me I'm a hard nut to crack!'

'You are, my love, you are. But I'm going to enjoy removing that brittle exterior.' He raised her arms gently and slid her sweater over her head, then lowered her back onto the settee. His gaze slid appreciatively over her body, naked from the waist up. 'You're even more beautiful than I remember. Promise you'll never reject me again. Please, Abbey.'

'I didn't reject you the last time—' she pouted teasingly '—or had you forgotten?'

'Oh, Abbey!' he groaned. 'What fools we mortals are.'

She laughed delightedly. 'Now I know I'm back where I belong. But you need to brush up on your quotations these days. It should be "What fools we mortals be".'

He kissed her. 'It's only one mistake.'

'I don't know about that. Helen told me you said I was hiding my talents under a bushel—'

'So everything I say to Helen is reported back to

you, is it? I'll have to be careful.' He bent to cover her lips with his so that she couldn't argue. When, only moments later, his bleeper sounded, they both looked at one another and laughed. He crossed to her phone and chatted quietly for a few moments. Then he returned to the settee and took her in his arms again, laughing delightedly.

'That was A and E at the General. They've got a medical student complaining of backache following a car accident earlier this evening. Because of who he is, they thought I ought to take a look. Guess what his name is?' He took the card she had given him earlier from his pocket and read out the name. 'Kevin Allen, BDS.' He chuckled. 'I can't wait to see his face.'

CHAPTER ELEVEN

'SHALL I come with you?' Abbey asked.

Max inclined his head and raised an amused eyebrow. 'Do you really think that's a good idea?'

'I suppose not but oh, Max, I wish you didn't have to go.'

Still grinning, he bent to kiss her lips. 'There's a turn-up. Usually you're pushing me away. I don't want to go either, but I can't really refuse. And after all the shocks you've suffered today I think it might be a good idea for you to get a good night's sleep.' He looked at his watch and laughed. 'What's left of it, anyway.

'Later today perhaps I can persuade you to accept one of my invitations at long last. How about joining me for an evening meal? Followed by who knows what delights?'

'Yes, please.' She leaned over and kissed him so that he could have no doubt that she meant it. 'But not too early, I'm afraid. I have a meeting with Mr Barratt and Bob Holland in the afternoon, so I'm not sure what time I'll be back from the Mercy.'

'Trouble?' he enquired sympathetically.

'No—not really. Mr Barratt will probably want to go over the auditor's report, but the main reason I'm summoned is to discuss a purchasing plan to cover both the hospitals. Mr Barratt imagines we might get larger discounts that way.'

'What do you think?'

'It might work in some instances but I think only in the basics. Otherwise it could cause problems when special items are needed urgently. Every consultant here likes a different make of surgical glove and the number of different sutures the theatre staff are asked for is unbelievable. Bulk buying there will certainly be an impossibility unless we can get you all to conform.'

'No doubt Mr Barratt will suggest that's the answer.'

'It would be, but I'd hate to suggest to any of you that you change. You've all been spoilt for far too long and I'd be lynched!'

Pretending that her words had hurt him, he captured her with encircling arms and asked, 'How can you, of all people, suggest such a thing?'

'Easily,' she laughed, raising her face to receive his kiss. 'Don't forget I've worked in theatres myself.'

He released her reluctantly. 'Stand up for your rights, love. Don't let Mr Barratt get his own way if you're not happy. Now I really should go and check my patient. Half past eight tonight be OK?'

She nodded happily and Max lingered an extra moment to kiss her again and then, covering her with her sweater, reluctantly left.

Abbey lay there for a few moments savouring her new-found happiness, then, having checked her watch to discover that it was after one in the morning, took herself off to bed where she fell into a contented sleep filled with dreams of Max.

She woke early and snuggled down under her duvet, unwilling to relinquish her dreams so soon. When she next surfaced, a wintry sun was attempting to clear the sharp frost of the early hours.

Even scraping the ice from the windscreen of her car could not dampen her happy mood and as she drove to work thoughts of Max buzzed insistently round in her head. She was excited by the thought of meeting up with him again.

'You look happy,' Jane told her when she brought

in the mail later that morning. 'In fact, you look like the cat who got the cream. What gives?'

Abbey smiled and shook her head, unwilling yet to share her news. 'It's just such a lovely morning.'

'I didn't think it was this afternoon's visit to the Mercy that could be making you happy. You *have* remembered your appointment there, haven't you?' she added as an afterthought.

'Yes, I've remembered. But I'm not going to let them get me down. I'm gradually pulling this hospital round into profitability and I'm confident I can deal with any queries they might have.'

The morning dragged. She had been so sure that Max would find an excuse to visit her that when he didn't she couldn't help the old anxieties surfacing. Was her erratic behaviour of the past few weeks making him suspect that his behaviour the previous evening had been injudicious?

Restlessly she wandered down to the ward level, ostensibly to check on the patients but also in the half-hope that Max would be there.

Discovering that he had done his round much earlier, she told herself that she must learn to trust him. He was a busy man who couldn't always do what he wanted, when he wanted, and, having already arranged what time he would pick her up that evening, what more did she want?

'All well?' she asked Penny as they met in the corridor.

'Yes. Well, almost all—apart from the patient admitted overnight. He's a pain in the neck literally!' She laughed. 'He was in a car accident and apparently has a whiplash injury, but he's making such a fuss.'

'Mr Darby's patient?' Abbey queried.

'Yes. I suppose because he's a dentist doing a medical degree Mr Darby views him as a colleague and has brought him in for rest and physio. I wish he hadn't bothered. He's more trouble than all the other patients put together.'

'I'll go and see him. Which room?'

'Twenty-nine.'

Abbey found it difficult to hide her amusement as she made her way along the corridor. Her knock was answered by an imperious, 'Come in.'

She pushed open the door. 'Hello, Kevin. I didn't expect to see you here.'

He was lying on top of the bed, a support collar round his neck and a sulky look on his face.

'Oh. It's you!'

Abbey smiled. 'I was sorry to hear about your neck. I gather it's very painful.'

'You can say that again. I don't think your Mr Darby believes me—or he's getting his own back for what I did to his car.'

'I can't believe that, Kevin. Mr Darby is very conscientious.'

'Perhaps you'd ask him if I can have some stronger painkillers, then?'

'You need to ask the nurses about that. I'm only an administrator, remember? No problem with your room or the food, is there?'

When he merely glared at her, Abbey added, 'I do hope you soon feel more comfortable.' She made a hasty exit and, closing the door behind her, found Max outside, grinning from ear to ear.

'That put him in his place, Abbey.'

'I can't believe—he never even asked if I had any ill effects from the accident, you know. He's got no thought for anyone but himself. What kind of a consultant is he going to make?'

'I hope someone will take him to task before he gets that far. I'm going to discharge him now. I just came in to check his X-rays and they are clear. I don't believe he has a genuine whiplash. It wasn't a rear-end collision and he didn't hit me with all that much force. I think he must just have a very low pain threshold. What he's like when playing rugby I can't imagine. Wish me luck. I'll tell you all about it tonight.'

Before entering Kevin's room, he gave her a wink that sent streams of tingling pleasure through her whole body.

Thinking about their meal together as she returned to her office, she decided that she had nothing to wear for such a special occasion. Perhaps if she left early enough for her trip to the Mercy she could look for a new outfit in the nearby shopping centre.

Her mind made up, Abbey decided to miss lunch and leave for the Mercy immediately. The thin sun was still shining and she decided that instead of eating she would search out a suitable outfit for their first real date this time around.

An hour later she was about to give the task up as hopeless when she tried on a jade-green jersey two-piece that did wonders for her figure and colouring.

After she had paid and the suit was safely wrapped, she checked her watch to discover that she had only ten minutes to get to her appointment at the Mercy. Not wanting to be late, she rushed across to her car and chivvied the engine into life.

She was approaching the main gates of the hospital when the traffic ahead was slowed by roadworks.

Swearing under her breath at the delay, she had pulled the car to a stop when her interest was caught by the car in front. It was a BMW the same colour as the one Max had lost.

She checked the number plate but, seeing that it was totally different, thought no more about it when the lights changed to green, until the car suddenly pulled into a lay-by and, as she overtook, she saw the dent in the driver's door that had occurred in the Spread Eagle car park.

Realising that it *was* Max's car, and that it had been given new plates to disguise it, Abbey debated what action she should take. If she waited to see which way it went she would be late for her appointment, and yet if she moved on to look for a telephone box to report it to the police the car might disappear without trace.

She decided to slow down and see if the BMW was about to move on. It swept past her almost immediately, and she was horrified to recognise at the wheel the jaunty lad that Mr Murray had insisted had attacked him.

Determined now not to let him out of her sight, she followed the car past the Mercy and out onto the road towards the hotel Max had taken her to.

Several miles further on, the car swung into a smaller road that suddenly narrowed down to a single lane. Even as she dithered about what to do the BMW swung across the narrow lane, blocking it completely.

'You interfering bitch,' the driver of the BMW leapt out and snarled at her. 'It was you that stopped me mugging that old geezer as well! I suppose you recognised me and that's why you're following me?'

'I'm not following you,' Abbey said in a weak voice. 'I'm on my way to the Mercy hospital.'

'Oh, yeah? Well, you're going the wrong way.'

'Please, I wasn't following you. I just lost my way,' she said in a small voice.

'Shut up, will you?' ordered her assailant. 'This is the big one and you're not going to spoil it as well.'

As she nervously asked him what he was talking about in an attempt to bluff her way out of danger, she received a thump in the back which knocked the breath from her body.

Unable to speak or fight, she felt herself being bundled into the back of her Fiesta, and it was at that moment she realised that if accomplices could be

summoned up so fast in such an isolated area she must
have stumbled on something very big.

His temper barely under control, Max lifted the
receiver and punched the memory recall button that
held Abbey's number.

He'd rung it several times since he'd called round
to collect her and found her flat empty. After all they'd
shared the previous evening, he couldn't believe that
she had stood him up. But what other explanation
could there be?

He banged the receiver down again and swore under
his breath as he tried to fathom her behaviour. OK,
he'd been late calling for her, but surely she accepted
the demands of his profession by this time? Or had
she never intended to be there? And, if so, why?

It just didn't make any sense. If she was annoyed
when he wasn't there on the dot, why hadn't she
bleeped him through the hospital instead of taking off
in a huff? If she'd meant even one word of what she'd
said the previous night, her behaviour was inexcusable.
All he could think was that she was trying to get her
own back.

He paced restlessly up and down his room wondering
what to do. There was no way he'd be able to sleep
without having this out with her first.

He rang the St Luke's switchboard. 'Can you tell
me if Miss Westray can be reached on her bleeper?'
he asked the duty porter.

'No, afraid not. She should have been, but the rota's
been altered. Sister Baker is on call instead. Do you
want me to bleep her?'

'No, thanks.'

Helen was the last person he wanted to discuss his
problem with. He tried Abbey's number once more,
but with no success.

Max suddenly recalled her connection with Jack

Wickham and rang his number, struggling to appear calmer than he felt.

'Jack, I'm trying to find Abbey Westray. I'm wondering if she might be with your son and his wife. Could you give me their number?'

'I can, but it won't help.' He chuckled. 'Ben's in hospital, coming home tomorrow. Cheryl's with me to make the arrangements. Abbey isn't with her, I'm afraid. Hang on a minute, though; I'll just check if Cheryl has any clue as to where she might be.'

He was back moments later. 'Sorry. No idea.'

'Thanks for trying, Jack. Is Ben all right?'

'He's undergoing trials of a new treatment and seems to take two steps forward and one step back. However, it's early days yet, and what we're looking for is a miracle, so all we can do is pray.'

'I'll join you in that. See you around some time, Jack.'

Determined now to find out what was happening, he rang the Mercy and spoke to the night receptionist.

'Would you know if Miss Westray, the St Luke's manager, is with you? I believe she had an appointment with Mr Barratt earlier.'

The young girl didn't think so. 'The admin offices are closed, so she won't be there and I'm sure she's not in the hospital.'

'Is there anybody there who would know what time she left?'

'I'll just check the security book.' Max heard papers rustling at the other end of the telephone.

'It doesn't look as if she came into the hospital at all. I'm sorry, I can't help you further.'

His simmering fury was replaced by a sudden shaft of anxiety. Perhaps her car had broken down, or, worse still, she'd had an accident?

Thanking the girl for her help, he rang off and immediately phoned the local police station. 'Have there been any car accidents between Bleasdon and the Mercy Hospital today?'

Receiving a negative reply, he cut the call and sat back in his chair to think.

Abby's car certainly wasn't outside the flat, but if she'd gone out to avoid him it wouldn't be. Inactivity was suddenly intolerable to him. He drove over to St Luke's to check if her car was there. It wasn't.

He took out his mobile phone and rang the Mercy again and spoke to the same girl as before. 'Could your security man check if Miss Westray's car is in your car park? It's a—'

'I'm glad you rang back, sir. I had to contact Mr Barratt's secretary and I asked about Miss Westray and it seems she didn't keep her appointment.'

An icy hand clutched at Max's stomach as he stammered out his thanks. Something *had* happened to Abbey. She was so keen to succeed as a manager that if she hadn't kept her appointment something awful *must* have happened. He imagined her lying helpless in a ditch.

He rang the police again and this time reported her missing. He finished by giving them the make and registration number of her car.

'We'll circulate all mobile units to keep an eye open for this car, but there's not much else we can do at the moment, sir. Adults often have a good reason for disappearing. She may not want to be found. However, we'll bear your report in mind.'

Certain that they weren't going to do anything immediately, Max felt frustration welling up inside him.

Undecided as to what he should do next, he wandered into the hospital reception area, where his eye was caught by the local news programme that the porter was watching on television.

There was little news of any interest, apart from

extensive coverage of an armed robbery that had taken place at one of the banks. He was about to wander away when the camera swung round to show the car that had been used in the robbery and then abandoned. It was a dark blue BMW. Similar to the one he'd had stolen from the Arbour Hotel car park. The police were asking for information about ownership.

As the camera panned, he was horrified to see the damage to the driver's door that had occurred in the Spread Eagle car park. He rushed to the desk and telephoned the police station again and told them that he was the original owner and that he had reported the car stolen a couple of weeks before.

The constable on the other end of the line was obviously laboriously filling in forms.

'The number plates have been changed, but I'm sure it's mine. I recognise the dent in the door.'

The constable was suddenly interested. 'Could you just wait a moment, sir, and I'll get someone to speak with you?'

Max waited impatiently for a couple of minutes, but he wasn't prepared to stand there indefinitely doing nothing when he was now sure that Abbey must be in trouble. He didn't know how, but he felt sure that the car and her disappearance must be linked. It was all too much of a coincidence.

He drove straight to the police station and banged the bell on the reception desk. A constable poked his head round a door.

'I rang a few moments ago about owning the BMW shown on the local news and I reported a Miss Westray missing earlier today. I'm sure they're connected and she's in some kind of danger.'

'What makes you think that, sir?' A plain-clothes officer had joined them.

'That BMW. Where was it found?' He wondered if he was going mad.

'Abandoned not far from the Arbour Hotel—'

'That proves it. My car was stolen from there and she was in that area when she went missing. I'm going to look for her—'

'Mr Darby, this is all speculation,' the plain-clothes man said, but Max ignored him. Action was needed. Action they seemed incapable of. So he would look himself.

He drove the hired Astra at speed to the spot the policeman had mentioned, keeping his eyes peeled for Abbey's Fiesta *en route*. The area was cordoned off.

'I'm sorry, sir; no one's allowed through.' A bored policeman barred his way.

'I'm looking for the driver of a blue Fiesta—she's missing.'

'If she's in these parts she'll soon be traced, sir. We're going through the area with a fine-tooth comb.'

Max hovered uncertainly by the barrier for a while, desperately wondering what could have happened— where Abbey could be and what he could possibly do.

'You can't do anything here. I should report her missing and leave it to us, sir,' the policeman told him.

'I've notified your colleagues. They don't believe me.'

Sure that Abbey must be somewhere in the vicinity, he wanted to remain nearby, and the only place he could think of was the Arbour Hotel itself.

He told the policeman where he was going and reluctantly drove back to the hotel, intending to find something to eat.

He was surprised when he had to park in the overflow carpark, but then he recalled that it was Friday evening. Not wanting to face the crowds, he sat down in the reception area and, after ringing through to St Luke's to tell the switchboard where he was, told the girl behind the desk that he was waiting for a phone call.

*　　*　　*

It was nearly two hours later when it came—two hours during which the inactivity had nearly driven him mad. He'd rung the police several times, only to be told there was no news of Abbey. He'd tried her home number over and over again, hoping against hope that it *was* all a mistake as the policeman had suggested, that he *was* putting two and two together and making five. But there was never a reply. He'd left messages everywhere as to his whereabouts, in case Abbey tried to contact him.

'Mr Darby—phone call,' the girl called. 'You can take it over in that booth.'

Max snatched up the receiver. 'Darby.'

'Hi. John Ambrose from the Mercy. I've been trying to contact you.'

Max was far from pleased to hear from him. 'Unless it's urgent I can't speak to you now.'

'I rather think it might be. We have a patient here I'd like your advice on.'

Max snapped, 'Can't your own orthopaedic man deal with it?'

'He could. But the patient would prefer you.'

'Look, John, I don't think—'

'Before you refuse, hear me out. You know the patient—she's the hospital manager at St Luke's—'

'Good God! Where is she? What's happened to her? John, what's the matter with her—?'

'One question at a time, Max. She's here at the Mercy and there's nothing wrong with her that a lot of TLC won't put right—'

Max didn't wait to hear any more. He banged down the receiver and raced out to his car. His thoughts were so active that he knew nothing about the journey to the Mercy until he found himself outside the front entrance.

John Ambrose met him on the doorstep. 'Calm

down, Max. The police are with her at the moment,
but I can assure you she's OK.'

'What's happened to her? Let me see her. Oh, God,
if anything's happened to her I'll never. . .' His words
trailed off miserably.

'This way—it seems she was held because she'd
recognised your car. It was used for a bank robbery.
She was released unharmed miles out in the country
and walked back—Bob Holland happend to be driving
that way and saw someone limping across a field in
the moonlight.'

'Limping?' Max's anxiety was getting the better of
him again. 'For goodness' sake! What have they done
to her?'

'She's sprained her right ankle—torn the ligaments,
I should say. That's all. Bob stopped because he
thought it was someone up to no good. He couldn't
believe his eyes when he discovered it was a
bedraggled Abbey.

'In here.' John poked his head round the door of one
of the Mercy's single rooms and beckoned a policeman.
'This is Max Darby, the orthopaedic consultant I told
you about. Can he come in for a moment? He won't
believe she's OK unless he can confirm it with his
own eyes.'

Abbey looked up to see Max striding across to the
chair where she sat and, oblivious of the onlookers,
he took her in his arms. 'Darling, darling Abbey. Are
you all right?'

At her breathless nod, he kissed her soundly and
murmured, 'What on earth happened? Did you confront them about the car? What—?'

'I'll ask the questions if you don't mind,' one of the
policemen interrupted gently. 'Now, if you're satisfied
that she's still in one piece, do you think we
could get on?'

Max released his hold reluctantly. 'Oh, Abbey, I'd never have forgiven myself if anything had happened to you.'

'We're trying to get a description of her assailants, sir. If you'll just wait outside and let me do that, we'll leave you alone. At least for the moment.'

When the police were at last satisfied with the descriptions she was able to give them and Abbey was happy with the picture they'd built up of the car driver who'd also attacked Mr Murray, they left.

Max rapidly came in to join her again. 'Now. Tell me everything that happened.'

'It was the lad who attacked Mr Murray who was driving your car. Mr Murray wasn't confused after all.' She burst into tears and he cradled her in his arms. 'I'm exhausted, Max. I just want to go home.'

Max was appalled. 'No way. That story is going to be headline news. And to think I stopped you going to the police! If that chap thinks you can recognise him. . .' He didn't finish his sentence but said, 'I'm not going to let you out of my sight for a moment. We need to find you a safe hiding place. The Arbour's not far from here. . .'

'I can't go to a hotel looking like this. Just take me home, please, Max.'

He hugged her tightly. 'No way. I've been nearly up the wall with worry already.' He kissed her gently. 'I know. If I take you home with me, Mum and Dad will be there for you if I should be called out.'

Abbey felt the colour rising in her cheeks. 'Max, we can't—your mum and dad! I don't know them.'

'Oh, yes, we can. I'm living with them at the moment until my new house is ready, but they won't mind.'

She looked up at him with tear-drenched eyes. 'If you don't intend to let me out of your sight, I imagine your poor mother and father will be horrified.'

He laughed. 'They won't be if I tell them we're

getting married just as soon as it can be arranged.'

'But Max, you haven't asked me.'

'I was going to. This evening. But you stood me up.'

Seeing the twinkle in his eye, she ignored his last remark. 'Shouldn't we get to know one another again first?'

He wrapped his arms around her tightly. 'Oh, Abbey, I do love you so. I don't need to know anything more about you.' He nuzzled her neck, then, the touch of his lips leaving a blazing trail across her cheek, gently nibbled her earlobe.

Abbey squirmed with desire as he told her, 'Thank goodness you *are* a hard nut to crack. I really thought I was never going to see you again.'

Abbey gazed up at him, tears welling in her eyes as the horrendous events of the day crowded in on her again.

'I'm sorry, love. Let's get you home. But first, what about this injury?' He took her ankle in his hands and his gentle probing belied the strength and size of his hands. 'How did you do it?'

Conscious that his touch was sending shock waves spinning through her body in all directions, she murmured, 'Climbing a fence—or, rather, falling off one.'

'Mmm—John might be a general surgeon but he knows a damaged ligament when he sees one. Let's see what I can find to support it.'

He disappeared but was soon back with a crêpe bandage. 'I've seen John and thanked him for all he's done. He's going to pass your thanks on to Bob as well.' Whilst speaking, Max applied the bandage firmly. 'Now, how does that feel?'

Abbey gingerly put her foot to the ground. 'Not too bad.'

'I'd suggest you lean on my shoulder if you could reach it. As you can't I'm going to sweep you off your feet. How does that sound?'

'Wonderful, Max,' she told him a moment later snuggling into his shoulder. 'This is where I belong.'

As he settled her into the Astra, he asked, 'Where's your car?'

Abbey shrugged. 'After I was dumped they made off with the Fiesta.'

Max roared with laughter. 'I'm not sure if I can afford to marry you after all. In a few short weeks we've got through three cars between us. I'm supposed to be exchanging this damaged thing for an Audi tomorrow. And to think before I met up with you again I'd never made a claim to an insurance company.'

'Neither had I,' Abbey told him indignantly.

'I'll have to give you the benefit of the doubt, then.' He kissed her again before starting the engine and driving off.

'You're taking a lot for granted. I haven't agreed to marry you yet,' she reminded him tearingly.

His first stop was to allow her to pick up some clean clothes from her flat. Before he allowed her out of the car, he took hold of both her hands. 'But you will, won't you?'

'Maybe. But not immediately. I'm just getting on top of things at St Luke's; I would hate anyone else to get the credit for my work.'

'Fine, but you did say over that meal at Melissa's that you would arrange a holiday once you were settled in—'

'Talking about holidays, how's Andy? Will he be able to go on his skiing holiday?'

Max was exasperated by her interruption. 'He's fine—he has youth on his side and there's no problem. I'm trying to talk about us, though, Abbey. I've arranged another two-week trip to India next month. That seems a suitable time for a honeymoon to me. And I won't object to you working on our return either—for a short while at least. How does that sound?'

'Wonderful. I feel better already.' When they'd disentangled themselves, she asked, 'Can't we stay here at the flat tonight? I want you all to myself and it won't be the same with your parents there. I'll be OK if you're here with me.'

'No way. I'm not taking the risk. I want you out of here just as soon as you've packed your bag.' He thought for a moment before saying, 'I suppose we could move into my new place. There is a bed, but it has precious little else in the way of comfort. You see, I'm waiting for someone to advise me on the decor!'

'Max Darby, is that the only reason you've asked me to marry you?'

'What do you think?' He kissed her again. And again, until her tingling senses refused to allow her to think straight. Momentarily pulling away from her, he grinned wickedly. 'You'll never know, will you?'

'And I don't care,' she told him.

After a night of lovemaking that left no doubt in either of their minds about their compatibility, they awoke late next morning to hear on the news that the suspected bank robber had been arrested along with his accomplices and they had all been remanded in custody for the weekend.

'If you don't mind, Max, I'd like to go and tell Mr Murray. He knew I didn't really believe him about the attacker.'

Max nodded. 'We'll call in on him on the way to see Mum and Dad.'

It was just as well they did. When they got to the house in Downs Road they found that Mr Murray had had a fall in the kitchen and this time he *had* displaced his new hip.

Abbey travelled with him to St Luke's in the

ambulance, while Max followed in his hired car.

Within an hour of them finding him Mr Murray was in the operating theatre again, with John Browning anaesthetising and Abbey and Ellie assisting.

After announcing that he and Abbey were to be married just as soon as it could be arranged, Max turned to her, his eyes twinkling above his mask. 'Ellie and John have been talking about it for months. We'll show them how to do it, shall we?'

Suddenly realising that Max's interest in Ellie must have been purely as a messenger to carry details of operation lists to John, she smiled up at him with her eyes and nodded.

Secure in his love for her, she now knew that every threat to her happiness with him had been in her own imagination. Conscious of her stupidity, she recognised, as Max must have done all those years ago, that loving someone meant putting their desires above your own.

She handed him the scalpel his outstretched hand was demanding and murmured, 'Whatever you say, Doc!'

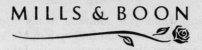

MILLS & BOON

MEDICAL ROMANCE

The books for enjoyment this month are:

MILLS & BOON

Back by Popular Demand

BETTY NEELS

COLLECTOR'S EDITION

A collector's edition of favourite titles from one of the world's best-loved romance authors.

Mills & Boon are proud to bring back these sought after titles, now reissued in beautifully matching volumes and presented as one cherished collection.

Don't miss these unforgettable titles, coming next month:

Title #5   OFF WITH THE OLD LOVE
Title #6   STARS THROUGH THE MIST

Available wherever
Mills & Boon books are sold

Delicious Dishes

Would you like to win a year's supply of simply irresistible romances? Well, you can and they're FREE! Simply match the dish to its country of origin and send your answers to us by 31st December 1996. The first 5 correct entries picked after the closing date will win a year's supply of Temptation novels (four books every month—worth over £100). What could be easier?

A	LASAGNE		GERMANY
B	KORMA		GREECE
C	SUSHI		FRANCE
D	BACLAVA		ENGLAND
E	PAELLA		MEXICO
F	HAGGIS		INDIA
G	SHEPHERD'S PIE		SPAIN
H	COQ AU VIN		SCOTLAND
I	SAUERKRAUT		JAPAN
J	TACOS		ITALY

Please turn over for details of how to enter ☞

How to enter

Listed in the left hand column overleaf are the names of ten delicious dishes and in the right hand column the country of origin of each dish. All you have to do is match each dish to the correct country and place the corresponding letter in the box provided.

When you have matched all the dishes to the countries, don't forget to fill in your name and address in the space provided and pop this page into an envelope (you don't need a stamp) and post it today! Hurry—competition ends 31st December 1996.

**Mills & Boon Delicious Dishes
FREEPOST
Croydon
Surrey
CR9 3WZ**

Are you a Reader Service Subscriber? Yes ❏   No ❏

Ms/Mrs/Miss/Mr _____

Address _____

_____

_____ Postcode _____

One application per household.

You may be mailed with other offers from other reputable companies as a result of this application. If you would prefer not to receive such offers, please tick box. ❏

C396
F